SUGAR

From barista to escort, life couldn't get any sweeter.

SUGAR

MILA HART

Edited by
WALLFLOWER EDITS
Cover by
VANILLA LILY DESIGNS

For the girls doing what they've got to do to make it.
Keep digging.

PEYTON

When Samantha looked down at the picture on my phone, a strange noise released from her throat with the lack of oxygen entering her lungs. "Holy shit, that man is freaking gorgeous." Her eyes bulged the longer she took in the image.

I laughed, taking back the phone to stare at the picture of the handsome man in his thirties for what had to be the tenth time. "I know, right? I told him to pick me up tonight in front of Cassie's parents' house. They live in that swanky neighborhood off of Fifth Street. I don't really want him to know where I live."

Sam nodded. "Yeah, I do that, too, when I meet new clients, just in case they're not all *there*. You know what I mean?"

I bit my lip and nodded. I was nervous, really nervous about tonight. "I still can't believe it, Sam. This has to be a catfish. Like, I'll bet you a dollar he's some old man with shriveled up balls and saggy boobs."

Sam snickered as she shook her head. "Ha, I'll gladly take it now if that's the case. This is legit girl. You already know I've been getting paid by *real* clients for a while. And I've yet to come across anyone who's lied or not been what they said they were."

I hummed distractedly as my thoughts strayed to some of the most horrific things my mind had dreamt up over the past few days. "Yeah, but with my luck, I wouldn't be surprised if he's some creep using someone else's photo. What if he locks me in his car so I can't get out? Oh my God, what if he traps me in his basement and forces me to do some creepy form of BDSM like letting him play with my eyelashes or something? I can't get pink eye Sam; it sucks! Eww, *shit*. What if he tries to make me eat his—"

"Okay, please stop." Sam gawked at me like I had grown a second head.

"I've done this for almost a year, and there have been no kidnappings and no strange fetishes. I haven't even taken off a *lick* of clothing since the day I started. Worst case scenario, I've been bored and watched the minutes on my watch tick by until it was over. And even then, I typically felt sorry for the guy."

I raised my brows at her, my arms flailing uncontrollably as they moved in a broad gesture. "Really, then why would they pay you in the first place?"

Sam snorted like a pig when I almost dropped my phone mid-sentence. "Not everyone's looking for a relationship, Peyton. A lot of these guys are influencers who just need someone to get the media off their backs and keep the women at bay."

That made sense. I was about to let it go when suddenly her words registered in my brain. "Wait a minute." It was like a flash of lightning that triggered the realization five minutes after it happened—I'm not always on the uptake. "You've been doing this for about a year now? If it's so great, why not tell me about it sooner?"

Sam rolled her eyes. Looking back on it, she probably suspected I'd act just like I had. "Because, you're a twenty-two-year-old-college student studying pre-law. Isn't there something in your classes about being all goody-goody, pristine, and shit? Don't you take some kind of oath like doctors?"

At that moment, my eyes were like daggers, and if they could cut a chick, I'd be in jail right now. Sam noticed that I was about to go on another tangent and snatched my phone before I could slip up again.

"I have been working six to eleven every morning at that crappy cafe for the past two years while juggling classes and homework. You know, that thing you shrug off so you can party with the next questionable dude, not to mention—"

Sam raised her hand to cut me off before I said anything I might regret. "Listen, I didn't tell you because I was still figuring it out myself. I wasn't so sure, either, all right." Her tone got cold, and for a petite blonde who barely reached five foot, she could be really damn intimidating. "And the truth is, I was a little uneasy about admitting I was an escort because just like you, everyone believes that means upscale prostitute. And I assure you, Peyton, I am not a whore."

I took in a deep breath. We both knew I was the one stepping out of line, yet I couldn't help but feel a bit betrayed. I hated my damn job, and there wasn't a day that Sam didn't hear exactly why. She also could've gotten hurt while doing this on her own, with no one having a clue where she was or whom she'd gone out with—that was a horrible thought to have. She was like a sister to me.

"Besides, the entire job description is being someone's arm-candy. I've known you for seven years Ton-Ton, and we both know you hate being objectified. Holy hell, it's basically the reason you hate your job in the first place."

My lip lifted into a sneer at the "loving" nickname she had given me in the ninth grade. "Well, *Sammy*, I don't hear about your getting called a *fat* piece of meat, slapped on the *ass,* and still being forced to serve a sack of shit when you're out on your little dates."

Sam shook her head as she looked around the room as if asking the air for a brain. "So, what, now you're defending *my* job? You don't even know much about it."

I furrowed my brows. "Were you not the one trying to convince me for the past *week* to download this Sugar Daddy app?"

"Yeah, so? And why the fuck are you yelling?" Sam shouted back.

"I don't know. Why the fuck are we fighting?" I could sense how wide my eyes had gone, and I could see her chest heave and nostrils flare—the two of us were pieces of work.

We both jumped when a loud bang hit our side of the wall, followed by our neighbor's scalding voice. *"Shut the fuck up!"*

Sam and I went silent as we looked at each other,

scared shitless. A moment passed before we burst into a fit of giggles, and the man in the apartment next to ours pounded on the wall again.

Once we'd calmed down, Sam checked a notification that popped up on my phone. Without a word, she stood and grabbed the small stack of clothes she'd placed for me by the edge of the couch. I sat up from my spot on the floor, not knowing how the hell I ended up there.

"Wait, I don't know if I want to do this."

Sam rolled her eyes, showing me the picture on my phone of the good-looking guy who expected to take me out in a few hours. "Trust me. With this face, you'll regret it if you *don't* go. Besides, he offered a thousand bucks for a single date. It's a few measly hours on the arm of a god."

I scrambled to get up after hearing that and slipped in my effort to race to my feet and almost face-planted the floor. "No way. You're not serious. Let me see." I squeaked, and Sam's smirk widened as she placed a hand on her hip.

"Why, I thought you weren't interested, little missy?" Sam's poor attempt at a Southern accent made me scoff.

"Yeah, well, that was before he added an extra five hundred dollars to the kitty."

She handed me the phone, and there in black and white sat the newly added bonus for me to keep his name and occupation out of my mouth and off the internet.

"Whoa, does this not sound suspicious to you? Some random dude wants me—a complete stranger—to be his date yet not tell anyone his name or where we're going. In what decade would that have ever been safe?"

Sam rolled her eyes, and I wondered how much longer I had before she totally lost her patience with me or her eyes stuck in the back of her head. "Peyton, he pays you through the website. They do thorough background screenings—remember all those blanks you bitched about filling out? The app researches both parties. Plus, all the information is on that app—from billing addresses to date location and times—if something were to happen to you, he'd be caught easily." She'd lost her damn mind.

"Yeah, *after* something bad happens."

Sam sighed. "Well, it doesn't really matter since you already told me everything about it. If you're not back on time tonight, I'll be the first to know." She shrugged as if she weren't sending me off to meet the grim reaper or straight into the mouth of the lion.

"Are you sure you can't just...follow us?" I gave her my best puppy dog eyes.

We stared at each other for what seemed like at least five minutes before she finally gave in. "Ugh, fine. Just don't say shit if I get caught."

My head bobbed in agreement as I headed for the bathroom, grabbing my clothes from her hands along the way. It wasn't until I had stripped down to my underwear that I noticed that the clothes Sam had picked out weren't mine. Nor had I ever seen them before. Whoever had chosen this had fabulous taste and deep pockets.

An hour had passed, and somehow, I'd managed to pull myself together. I stood in front of the mirror, shocked by my final appearance. The transformation from a mousy pre-law student to a smoldering knockout blew me away. I almost didn't recognize myself—it was amazing what expensive clothing did for a girl with a little meat on her bones. Sam banged on the door, knocking me out of my trance, and I made my way out of our apartment hot on her heels. As soon as I got into Sam's car, she sent me a low whistle of appreciation.

"Damn, no need to thank me. The way you look in that outfit is thanks enough."

I laughed, shaking my head. It was no surprise that even the compliments Sam gave were narcissistic. Although I had to admit, she'd done well with the short blue dress that felt like it was silk. And with the matching high-heeled stilettos that somehow reflected the shadows themselves, I was suddenly four inches taller. I looked longer and leaner, and I felt like a million dollars. I guessed if I was going to meet my maker at the hand of a stranger, doing so in style was the best way to go. This dress would forever be magic in my mind.

I held up the sparkling purse made of what looked to be real diamonds—although I was certain it wasn't—in Sam's line of sight. "How?"

One question was all it took to get my bestie to spill the details. "A client bought me those clothes for one of our dates. He wanted to impress his brothers, show them that he could catch a beauty such as *moi*." Sam flipped her naturally curly hair as she turned on the car's GPS and linked it with the location on my phone.

"I thought it was weird in the beginning, you know," not taking her eyes off the road as she talked, "that he couldn't get a date on his own. Even ugly men can get a date without paying chicks to spend time with them. I mean, the dude was pretty hot. But less than an hour into our first date, it all made sense when I realized he was gay."

I lifted a brow in amusement; Sam's stories were always entertaining, to say the least. "Really, what exactly led you to that conclusion?"

Sam shrugged. "It was kind of obvious. He was uncomfortable, but not nervous, more like he didn't have a clue what to do. And his brothers mentioned that he had always stayed away from girls like they were the plague in high school. *And,* let's not forget to mention how conservative that dress is."

I snorted. "That doesn't mean he's gay, Sammy."

She gave me a smug look and narrowed her eyes in irritation. She hated Sammy as much as I hated Ton-Ton. "And which one of us is better at reading people?"

I tried not to laugh in her face but ultimately failed. "Considering how bad we both are at relationships, I'd say neither."

Sam huffed, as she made another turn. We sat in silence for a while, but I still had worries popping up in my head.

"Have you had any crazy experiences so far?"

Sam glanced at me from the corner of her eye before responding. "Nah, I've had a few sketchy personalities here and there, but my clients have been pretty nice. More often than not, they just need someone to serve as a place holder for events. A hired 'plus one.'"

The answer released some of the unknown tension built up in the back of my neck. If anyone tried to hurt Sam, I'd have to go on a rampage. But she seemed pretty casual about the whole thing, and I considered the fact that I might be overreacting.

"He said he'd pick me up in a *limousine*, Sam. That alone is insane. I'm still expecting some old fat dude driving a convertible."

Sam shrugged as she messed with the radio. "More fun to see the look on your face when you're wrong then."

She blasted heavy metal as we arrived in Cassie's parents' wealthy and *quiet* neighborhood. She was trying to piss me off, and I knew it. One, it did nothing for my anxiety, and two, the growls and screams made the words so incomprehensible that I had no idea how anyone could understand what they said, much less call it music.

I immediately turned off the radio so we wouldn't get a complaint. I didn't want to be seen by these people. Dressed up or not, this was unfamiliar territory, and most of them probably wouldn't hesitate to call the cops. As much as I dreamed of a guy in uniform, I didn't care to be hauled off to jail in my magic dress and fuck-me heels.

Sam parked five houses away from the address I'd entered into GPS. I climbed out, careful not to ruin my dress or stumble in my shoes as I got to the curb. Once I'd straightened the skirt and checked my reflection in the car's window, I stuck in my head about to say bye to Sam. I pulled out my phone and searched for her contact.

"I'm going to call you so you can hear our conversation. Be sure to mute yourself."

Sam narrowed her eyes in exasperation but answered the call anyway. "And what exactly are you going to do when your battery dies?" she asked.

I smiled, answering her question by grabbing the spare block charger in her glove box. "Be sure to follow us," I said before shutting the door and hastily making my way in front of the two-story house where I asked him to pick me up.

I took deep breaths as I waited on Cassie's parents' porch, and I tried not to think about the windows in the houses around me. The lights were off, but it didn't make me feel any less paranoid that there could be someone watching me stand out here like a moron—or mistake me for a prostitute.

After five minutes, the paranoia set in, and I

started to chicken out. Then, a black streak came into my peripheral view, and I held my breath. *Oh my God, it's real.* I couldn't believe my eyes. I was so dazed that I flinched when the phone buzzed in my hand.

Sam: *Told you!*

A rush of adrenaline passed through me as I read Sam's text. The limo had stopped, and the driver's side opened as an old man in a grey suit stepped out. My face paled; he looked nothing like the man in the photo online. I stepped out of the shadows on the porch and onto the sidewalk so it appeared I'd come out of the house.

"Hello, Ms. Sanders. Mr. Hollens is waiting for you inside." The man spoke before I could yell out my thoughts, and thank God for that.

I had been so close to making a scene that no one would ever let me forget. I snapped my mouth shut to keep from gaping when the chauffer opened the rear passenger door for me, only for my jaw to drop again— I managed to keep my lips sealed—in shock. The man in the back seat was ten times hotter than should've been possible, and somehow, he made the image online look bad.

Heat rose in my cheeks as I took the seat next to

him. I wasn't expecting the cushions to be so comfortable, yet it wasn't enough to distract me from the Adonis who sat beside me. He wore a black suit, and his short, dark-brown hair sported a messy style. But it was his perfect nose and chiseled jaw that really highlighted his handsome features.

When I heard the first words that moved past those unbelievably soft-looking lips, I immediately knew this man was both a blessing and a curse. The sheer amount of control I was losing over my body would end up making me look like an idiot.

I shook my head, my face heating in embarrassment. "I'm so sorry. I spaced out for a second."

He chuckled, tilting his head in a way that reflected the light off of his beautiful hazel eyes. And I swear, my heart stopped and came back a zombie because it hadn't seemed to function quite right after.

"I said, you look beautiful, Peyton," Jake repeated, sending me another brilliant smile.

I fought every urge in my body to prevent myself from looking down at his mouth like some creep in a movie. I smiled back; unfortunately, I couldn't stop the slight quiver in my lips or the stutter in my voice as I responded. "T-Thanks, you're not too bad yourself." My face grew uncomfortably hot as my voice raised to a pitch too high for my liking.

Jake didn't seem bothered, but I suddenly regretted the fact that I still had Sam on the phone. If I took it out now, he'd notice, and that extra five-hundred was sure to go back into the pocket of his well-fitted trousers. Not that I was looking *anywhere* near there.

I'd gone mute, and I wanted to slap myself. I was my own worst enemy.

"Sorry about the inconvenience; the charity gala is still about an hour from here. I hope you don't mind."

I shook my head, quick to reassure him. "No, it's all right, plus, I get to check out this expensive limo, so it's cool."

Jake's smile tensed, and I quickly re-evaluated my words. My eyes scrunched closed in embarrassment as I covered my face and groaned into my hands.

"Oh my God, that sounded so...gold-digger-ish." My words were muffled by my palms. I lifted my head and looked him in the eyes. "I'm sorry. I'm nervous. This is my first time..." I trailed off. I had a horrible habit of reverting to an ignorant, uneducated tart when I got anxious.

Jake burst into laughter, and I slowly lifted my head in surprise as I watched him grab his stomach as he eased himself into low chuckles. "You're really cute. You know that?"

I would say that I blushed, but with how heated my face already felt, I doubted anyone would've been able to tell. "Hopefully that's a good thing." I grimaced as he smirked back at me and nodded.

"I'm guessing this is a new experience for you? Would you like to mess with the window controls? Play with the television remote?" Humor danced in his eyes, and I could tell he was being playful and not mean. "Would you like to check out the mini-fridge?"

My smile widened. "No way. You've got food in here?" My cheeks hurt from the grin that remained plastered to my lips.

Jake appeared enamored by my naïveté and curiosity, and it was clear we'd both started to loosen up. I couldn't stop the swell in my chest when it occurred to me that I was responsible for the smile that lit up his exquisite face.

He reached between us and opened a concealed compartment that held canned drinks and snacks. I took the can of sparkling cider he offered, and when our hands brushed, I swear it was better than all the romantic comedies on the planet. Whoever the poor soul was that came up with the whole "spark" thing obviously hadn't met the right person. Touching Jake was like having my hand incinerated from the inside out—in the best possible way.

Did I just meet my soulmate? Was this some kind of sign? Nah, those words didn't cross my mind. What did was, *this is it.* This was what women dreamed of and movie directors were desperate to portray. It wasn't just chemistry; it was electric—cosmic. I had *no* doubts.

I tried to focus on Jake's words; I honestly did. But he already had me questioning reality itself. Mentally, I needed to smack myself and stop dreaming. I would never have to worry about a second date if all I did was drool—he'd think I was a window licker with serious issues.

"Thanks." I popped the top on the can, careful not to mess up my freshly manicured nails or spill anything on this insanely expensive dress.

Jake eyed me curiously from my side. "You don't really seem the type to do this kind of thing."

I shrugged as I messed with the can, occupying my idle fingers. "That obvious, huh?" I didn't take it as an insult; in fact, I should have assumed it was a compliment. "You're right, though. This is my first... assignment."

His dark brow quirked along with his kissable lips. "Looks like we have something in common then."

It was my turn to show surprise. "Really? You haven't told me why you needed a date. Recent break up?" *Open mouth, insert foot.* I took a long sip of my drink to swallow that embarrassment.

He shook his head, but thankfully, he didn't seem at all offended by my lack of finesse. "I've got a lot on my plate right now. It's not really the best time to be in a relationship."

I nodded. "Yeah, I understand that," I said, trying not to sound exasperated. The number of essays that currently sat uncompleted on my desktop made his statement easy to relate to. Dating and pre-law did not go hand in hand, although neither did law school and a crappy job at a run-down café, which was what I faced next year if I didn't make some changes.

Jake averted his eyes, and his supple features suddenly went tense. "My father's going to be at the gala. He wants me to find someone to settle down with, but, I'm just not ready for that." He opened a can and took a sip of cider, undoubtedly collecting his thoughts. "At least not in the way he wants it to happen."

Jake's scent reached my nostrils as the air conditioner wafted the fragrance in my direction. It was subtle yet powerful, and I didn't notice how much it had drawn me toward him. That was until my finger grazed his again, and that electricity alerted me that we'd ended up sitting closer together. What started as almost three feet had been reduced to about twelve inches. He didn't seem to mind the close proximity, and that encouraged me to continue the conversation.

"Man, it would be tough to be a kid with a parent pushing for a relationship you're not interested in." Apparently, I really liked the taste of my toes since I kept inserting them into my mouth. I shouldn't offer my opinion on family affairs I knew nothing about.

The glimmer in Jake's eyes told me he found me amusing, despite myself. "First of all, *kid*, really? I'm like a decade older than you."

I lifted the can to my lips, shielding my mouth from view and my brows rose. "And second?" I waited for him to make another point.

He shook his head with a smirk. "I don't have a second point. I was hoping that *one* would be good enough."

I didn't try to hide my laughter. Jake had put me at ease, which would make the remainder of the night bearable, if not enjoyable, and I could stop talking like an idiot without a filter. The rest of the drive, we shared little facts about ourselves. Jake's favorite color was silver, and he tended to be a workaholic. Nothing we talked about was terribly personal, and even though I agreed with him when it came to holding off on relationships, I couldn't help but want to learn more about the man next to me.

I hadn't expected him to be playful or witty, likely because of the clout his name and company held. I'd anticipated being bored with a man ten years older than me. I didn't tend to surround myself with people outside of my age bracket. Forget that I was in college and everyone I knew was a law student—other than Sam, and I had no idea what her major was this month. I just had vastly different goals and values than someone in their thirties. But Jake's personality and his fun-loving spirit made him seem younger than his age. Although, it was impossible to miss the maturity that kept his mouth closed when I inadvertently opened mine and kept his eyes from going wide at the stupid things I said to his life experience that I wasn't privy to.

I was definitely overthinking things. All we'd done was sit in the back of a limo.

2

JAKE

I had to remind myself to breathe the first time I caught a glimpse of her. I was amazed at her beauty. And when she attempted to get to know things about me that no one cared to learn, an overwhelming warmth settled into my chest. I didn't make a habit of analyzing my feelings, nor did I do it in this case, but it was nice to chat with someone about insignificant facts that didn't require a multi-million-dollar decision at the end of the discussion or a check with name and bank account attached to it.

The moment I noticed we were at the charity gala, nausea swarmed in me like an angry hive of bees.

"Are you all right?" She pressed the back of her hand to my forehead. "You look pale, and you got quiet all of a sudden." Peyton's concern was sweet and unlike anything I'd experienced.

The forced grin I offered her was far more familiar than the carefree smiles she'd received throughout the ride. Feigning happiness and remaining poised was what I'd been trained to do my entire life. In the world I'd grown up in, everyone wore a mask and hid their discomfort. It was amazing how comfortable Peyton and I had gotten in each other's presence in the span of sixty minutes. "Yeah, we're here. Are you ready?" I asked, resisting the urge to sigh.

I had already told her about my dad's standards so she knew to act just a level below them to make this entire thing *believable*. I hated asking her to fall victim to him, but it was what I'd paid for handsomely. I could already see his tall figure waiting for us outside of the entrance, likely scaring the other contributors away.

"I'm a bit nervous about meeting your dad, but I think we'll be alright." Peyton's hands turned over themselves in her lap, but other than that one sign, I'd never know she was anxious. Her blue eyes sparkled, and she had just the right amount of smile to appear happy but not trying too hard. And damn, her legs went on for miles. I had to stop myself from acknowledging all her luscious curves, or we'd never get out of the limo.

My lips twitched upward at the word "we'll," and I wasn't entirely sure why, but before I had time to consider the way my heart beat and heat flowed through me, we stepped out of the limousine. Even the fresh air couldn't keep my father's presence from constricting around me like a snake. His critical stare bore holes through my flesh and made me want to crawl away in hopes he hadn't seen me.

"*Yikes*, there's someone who looks like they know karate," Peyton whispered into my ear as she walked close to me, her arm linked with my own.

I pursed my lips, but the desire to laugh was so strong that I slapped a fist over my mouth and pretended to cough. My father appeared anything but amused, though I was positive he hadn't heard her. His gaze settled on Peyton's in an appraisal that had my haunches raised and my defenses high. And then his sights focused on her arm linked with mine.

"And who might you be?" He demanded more so than asked and did so in a tone that didn't invite anything other than a straight answer.

"Hello. I'm Peyton." With the grace of a well-bred woman, she extended her hand in introduction, but he just stood there, glaring pointedly at our connected arms.

"And your last name?" he quipped, and I had to restrain the frustrated groan that wanted to slip past my lips.

"Sanders." Peyton didn't miss a beat, nor did she drop her eyes. Her gumption impressed me as she stood firm and squared her shoulders the way those in society did. Either she'd spent her fair share of time around up-tight assholes, or she was a damn-fine actress.

I quickly chimed in to the conversation when Peyton shifted beneath his glare. "We've been dating for a few months, and I thought you'd like to meet her." I forced myself to relax not only my posture but my tone as the lies flew from my mouth. There was something about Peyton that made it easy to be around her, and even simpler to pretend we'd been doing it for weeks.

My father gave me a suspicious look, the same one he used to reserve for my mother, who had believed a lie among friends was nothing more than an offer of peace in polite society. I kept my gaze steady, preparing myself for whatever harsh statement came from his mouth next. I let out the small breath I was holding when Peyton sank into my side. The heat of her body next to mine gave me comfort—like we were a team—in this suffocating situation.

"*Sanders* isn't a family name that runs in our circle, Jake." He sneered Peyton's last name as though it were vile, leaving no misunderstanding about what he'd meant.

"Dad!" My tone left zero room for interpretation. I hadn't expected him to say something so rude. Harsh, yes, but insulting a complete stranger rather than his own son, was a first even for him. Since there had been no mention of legally binding ties like marriage, her family name meant nothing in this situation—or any other in my mind.

Peyton furrowed her brows, and something shifted in her expression. She was no longer the witty, quirky, and slightly awkward young woman who'd sat next to me for the last hour. Something akin to fury ignited in her eyes, and her hold on my arm tightened. Peyton wasn't about to let anyone dismiss her, regardless of their last name or hers.

"Excuse me, sir, my last name or the social circle it might be associated with has no bearing on my worth or potential. To make such an assumption toward someone you've just met is terribly disrespectful." Her voice remained strong and steady, and she never diverted her gaze away from my father's eyes.

I went rigid as his glare increased, and the lines around his eyes and mouth deepened. I was quite impressed actually. The way she'd spoken and carried herself earlier was rather casual, but now I could tell that she could be authoritative whenever she wanted—or needed—to be. The woman had more class in her pinky than my father had in his entire body.

"Teach your woman some manners, Jake."

I kept my expression carefully stoic and squeezed Peyton into my side when I saw her lips part to retort. The incredulous look she sent me was adorable, and although I couldn't blame her, the man was still my father. It wouldn't benefit either of us to rile him any further, and I didn't need the press would catch wind of a scene in front of the gala. It was easier to shake his hand and leave.

In a way, calling her "my woman" was his way of accepting her. It was rude, but I caught the true meaning behind his words because I'd dealt with him my entire life. Nothing he ever said really meant what came out. Innuendo and implication were a language unto themselves in the Hollens world.

My father grunted before heading inside the building packed with people. They all wore expensive suits and dresses, and many held wine glasses. Peyton had an air of wonder about her, or maybe it was subtle appreciation. I'd be the first to admit, it was cute the way her face lit up as she took in everything around her. And when she spotted a celebrity, she inhaled deeply and might have danced just a bit on her toes, but she regained her composure, and aside from that barely noticeable slip, she never let on that this was anything special. I didn't know anything about her family name or where she came from, but she had no problem mingling. Gone were the nervous slip-ups that I'd seen in the limo when I'd first picked her up, and at my side stood a woman who acted like she'd been here for years.

We walked through the crowd, pausing every couple of moments to greet the people who knew me in various ways.

"Oh, dear, look at you! I see you've finally started dating again."

I gave Mrs. Patterson a tight smile and nodded. This was precisely why I hated coming to these things. I didn't mind donating; I hated being under a microscope. Not even having a woman on my arm kept nosey old ladies from running their mouths. Now wasn't the time for this discussion, and when I tried to reroute our course, I caught my father staring at us from the corner of the room. I wished my sister were here to distract him, but alas, she was too busy with her own social engagements to worry about mine.

Somewhere along the way, Peyton and I had found ourselves with glasses of champagne. I took it out of her hand the moment she put the glass to her lips.

"Wha—" Her pouty lips begged to be bitten, but I refrained.

"Trust me, you want to have all of your faculties at full strength for this evening," I whispered into her ear, and the huff she let out in protest made my dick twitch.

I placed the glasses on the tray of the next server we passed, both left untouched. My father didn't need another reason to scold me, not that I wasn't in my thirties or anything. We made our way to the large, padded chairs in the center of the room when the host took to the podium. Peyton moved her hands between us as if she were inspecting the seats.

"Wow, these are soft." Her hushed whisper was as cute as she was, and I smirked as she adjusted herself to sit more comfortably. She glanced up, and I took note of the fact that my father sat quite some distance away from us.

"Your dad's not terribly approachable."

I huffed out a laugh at her restrained evaluation. "You haven't even seen the worst of it."

She looked at me, horrified. I just gave her an exasperated look with a shrug of indifference. We went quiet as soon as the host on stage began to speak.

"I'd like to thank you all for attending. Your generous donations will be greatly appreciated by programs such as STF and FDV."

Saving the Family was a program geared toward helping third-world children and families living in poverty. Their sister foundation, Fight Domestic Violence, was designed to lend a helping hand to struggling men and women to escape the threats they faced in their homes and immediate environments. Both were close to my heart, and I attended the gala annually.

"Our goal tonight is to raise six million dollars to support the causes these programs represent." The host continued, but I found myself taking note of Peyton.

Her interest appeared piqued, but what surprised me was the twinge of guilt that flashed across her expression when the servers handed us each a piece of paper with directions on how to donate electronically.

"You can donate using my name or anonymously if you wish." My chest clenched as I witnessed her anguish mar her beauty. I put my hand on top of hers, hoping it would ease whatever tension had consumed her. "The amount raised will be displayed on the screen, along with our goal." I didn't know how to tell her she didn't have to donate without offending her, yet I recognized that if she were on the Sugar Daddy app, it wasn't because she was independently wealthy.

The host finished, and before Peyton could over-think it, I found myself snatching the paper from her hands. She looked at me, questioningly, and I just smiled.

"Don't worry about it," I whispered and put in our donations. Two million instantly showed across the screen, and her grip tightened on my hand as she slowly looked from the screen to my phone.

Peyton didn't speak. She didn't need to. Her eyes said it all. I didn't know her circumstances, but it showed in her expression how generous she believed the contribution to be. But I didn't give to impress her; I gave because it was the right thing to do.

By the time the event was over, my father had decided to harass us once more before informing me that I had to be in Australia with my sister tomorrow afternoon and then France the following week. Appar-ently, there were meetings regarding our hotel chain that he had decided I must attend at the last minute—it didn't escape my attention that he stared Peyton down as he delivered the news. I no more needed to be at those meetings than Peyton did, but it was his way of putting distance between us—his form of a test of our "relationship." If only we had one.

I glanced at Peyton as we approached the limo. She looked as worn out as I felt.

"We need to drive straight to the airport." I barely knew the girl, and I hated what I had just put her through. And it wasn't over. "I know it's out of the way, but unfortunately, I can't miss the flight."

She nodded. "It's all right; I understand." There was something on the tip of her tongue, but whatever it was, she decided not to voice it. The emotion in her eyes passed just as she looked away.

"So, what did you think of tonight?" I asked as I held open the door for her to get in. I waved absent-mindedly to people who caught my attention before getting in behind her.

"Well, aside from your father's surly disposition, it wasn't all that bad." Her tender smile remained in place, and I realized she was no worse for wear. She'd endured like a champion, and I was rather proud to have had her on my arm all night.

"You get used to it after a while."

"I feel like vampires sucked the life out of me." That part never changed, sadly. "It's like you're always performing."

"Now you know why they all go so far to look generous."

Peyton giggled. "Well, whether it's for the recognition or not, it helps either way. That's all that matters in my book," she said softly, once again looking at me with her stormy blue-grey eyes. When she was happy, they were the color of the ocean; when she was reticent, they were slate and dangerous.

I couldn't help but find my gaze trailing across her pale skin, taking note of the freckles that peppered her perfect complexion. Her light brown hair held an intricate braid that fell to the middle of her back. I had no idea why, but it was like noticing her for the first time all over again—except in greater detail. "Beautiful." The word slipped past my lips before I realized I'd spoken.

"Thank you." Her timid tone soothed my aching spirit, and her eyes fluttered as the two of us moved forward.

I hadn't noticed how close we'd gotten until the warmth of her breath pressed against my mouth, and suddenly, I found mine touching hers as I fell deeper into her. Her lips were softer than they appeared, and I hummed in approval. Nibbling at her lower lip, I tasted the sweetness of her blueberry Chapstick, and her hands started to roam beneath the hem of my shirt as she eased it from my pants.

I placed my hands on her thighs as I brought her into my lap, and she gasped when she felt my erection press against her panties. That was all it took for me to slip my tongue into her mouth. She was warm, and the moment my tongue pushed against hers, I felt a shiver of pleasure run down her spine. When we pulled apart for breath, I went in for her freckled neck, reaching over with my hand to undo her zipper and bra. I didn't want the moment to end, and I didn't believe either of us wanted to think too much about what we were doing. So, we didn't.

I sucked a trail of affection across her collarbone and down as I exposed her breasts to the cold air. My calloused hands trailed tenderly over her pert nipples before pinching her slowly. And when her head fell back, I captured a taut peak in my mouth and teased her with my tongue.

She squirmed beneath my touch, and I was still very much aware of the weight above my dick. Her hips rolled like she was desperate to get friction between her thighs. I tugged at Peyton's hair as my nails dug lightly into her thigh. But when she stopped moving, and I dared to make eye contact, it was the devilish smirk on her face that had me ready to tear into her.

I grunted or maybe growled before I found myself replacing it with a groan as she swiftly unbuckled my belt and unzipped my pants. She slid them off along with my boxers. I let her up, so she could take off her panties, and I watched unashamedly as Peyton bent over, letting the dress slide from her hips. The curves of her plump ass made my mouth water as she slipped off her dark-laced thong.

"What are you—" I started to say, when instead of mounting me immediately, she pushed me down onto the seats. I let out a shuddered breath the moment she grabbed my throbbing cock and slipped it into her mouth.

I hardened between her lips as she placed her hands firmly around my sack and massaged my balls with her thumb. I could feel a tremor of pleasure dance throughout my body, and deep breaths soon turned into pants. "O-oh my God." I gasped, and all the blood rushed straight into my dick. I curled my toes when she let my cock slip out of her mouth all too soon.

A moment passed, and I was able to clear my mind enough to take a condom out of my wallet. Peyton took it from me, slightly surprised, but she didn't hesitate to slip the latex down my shaft, and then she kissed her way up my abs. Her touch was as tantalizing as it was teasing. When she reached my neck, I inhaled the scent of her hair, again finding the hint of blueberries. And then...she slipped my cock inside her pussy.

She slowly began to rock her hips in slow, circular motions as she latched her teeth into the side of my neck. I wasn't sure what felt better, her lips on my skin or the way she gripped me from the inside out—fuck she was tight. Her legs quivered against my thighs, and I rolled her onto her back across the seat, switching our positions. It took seconds to find her eyes, and no matter how hard I tried, I couldn't break our stare. Her heels dug into the backs of my thighs, prompting me to move faster, deeper, harder. I rounded my hands around her shoulders for leverage and tucked my face into the curve of her neck where I lavished her with kisses.

"Oh, yeah, *fuck*." She panted, and I smirked.

The more noise she made, the harder I pounded into her, taking her, claiming her, dominating her. The muscles in Peyton's legs flexed, gripping me, and I didn't even try to stop the roar that echoed past my lips and into the back of the limo. My heart pounded erratically, but it wasn't enough.

"*Shit*, say something dirty!" Peyton moaned as she

dropped her head back, her breasts bouncing freely with the arch of her back. Damn, she was perfection.

The sounds of our colliding together clapped throughout the limousine. I didn't even care that Wilfer could most certainly hear what was going on behind him; it just turned me on that much more.

"You're fucking *hot!*" I couldn't think straight, much less formulate some erotic poetry to tickle her fancy.

She grabbed a fistful of my hair roughly and brought my head down to her face; my eyes widened, once again surprised by her show of authority. Her voice was delirious with pleasure—raw and husky. "You call that dirty? I just sucked your cock like a slut, and that's all you've got to say?"

I grinned like the Cheshire cat. My hips still moved as our breaths became more labored. Something stirred inside me, lighting a flame that had never burned. "Your pussy's so fucking tight I can't think straight."

"You're so *thick.*" The light in her eyes was animalistic and feral, and then she growled.

I couldn't say for sure that it was the hitch in my grind or the patch of gravel we'd hit on the road, but whatever the fuck it was, this was the best feeling of my life. It was more than closing a multi-million-dollar deal or the pleasure I got from seeing profits triple in a quarter—Peyton had gotten inside me.

She lifted her hips fast. It was so sudden that it jarred me from my thoughts, and I slipped so deep inside of her that we became one and the sudden rush of release overwhelmed me. Desperate for oxygen, I panted, allowing the precious air to enter my lungs, and with each gasp, euphoria washed over me. My face flamed with the burn of ecstasy.

"That was—"

"Surreal," she finished.

I pulled out, and we used the tissues in the built-in dispenser between the seats to clean up. We were in the middle of tugging on our clothes when my pocket buzzed. I checked the text on my phone. My sister, Jessica, was blowing me up with alerts about our departure. I had five minutes left to get on the plane, and I currently still sat in the limo on the tarmac.

I cursed mentally as I buttoned the last few holes on my shirt. We had been at the airport—I didn't know how long—and I had to sprint out of the vehicle to make my flight. I kissed Peyton's cheek like she hadn't just been the best lay of my life and flung open the door.

"Jake?" It was the last thing Peyton said as I dashed

toward the waiting plane without so much as a goodbye.

I couldn't slow down to tell her how amazing she was or how much I wanted to get to know her. I felt like shit leaving like I did, but if I missed this flight, not only would my dad have my head, but I'd likely be out of a job and my inheritance. Jessica waited at the bottom of the stairs onto the plane, holding our bags as she sent a glare my way, urging me to run faster.

"Hurry the hell up, Jake!" she shouted, and I sped up, making it in the last minute.

It was times like this that I wondered what the point was in having a private jet if we didn't get to operate on our own schedule. When we finally got settled next to each other, I noticed the strange way my twin stared at me.

"What?" I asked, and she sneered.

"Why the hell do you smell like sex?"

I blushed, ignoring her question as I quickly turned my head toward the window, watching the ground as the plane began to take off.

My mind didn't once stray from the young woman I met on the app and had just taken in my limo....

3

———

PEYTON

I was left in stunned silence the entire way home. A sick churning mulled in my gut as I considered the way he'd ignored me and raced toward the plane and the woman standing at the base of the steps. There wasn't so much as a goodbye, as if I didn't even exist after what we had just done. I clenched my fists around my purse as I began to direct my bubbling anger toward myself. I had no excuse for my poor decision—alcohol hadn't even played a factor.

I felt like a whore, and yet I'd decided to have sex with him regardless of the job. To make matters worse, Sam was late, and I was left standing outside for almost an hour in an unfamiliar neighborhood in my unkempt attire before she finally showed up. I likely looked like the poster child for date rape, and I didn't even care.

"Where the hell have you been?" I threw out the question before I'd finished sliding into the passenger seat. Once I buckled my seatbelt, I glanced over to see why she hadn't answered.

Her top lip was turned up in a sneer, and I worried if she opened her mouth, she might breathe fire. Sam was a bit disheveled, and I was fairly certain I saw her sock in the back seat. "I don't want to talk about it." Fire didn't blow into the air, but she was hot about something.

I furrowed my brows as I inched away from her sour attitude, doing my best to protect myself from potential backdraft. "Uh, okay...."

"So, you two looked rather cozy." She quickly switched the topic.

"Yup, all part of the job." I reached for the radio, hoping to cut the conversation short—and act like I was really that casual about what had happened—but Sam slapped my hand away.

"*Oh, really?* So, you have no feelings for that dude whatsoever?" She needed to grab a Kleenex to wipe off the sarcasm that dripped from her lips, but since I didn't have one, I kept my face angled toward the passenger window.

My cheeks flushed, and the heat that crept across my face became uncomfortable when I suddenly remembered my phone. I cringed as I reached for it in my purse, and then I prayed as I peeked at the call. If I could have kissed Jesus square on the lips at that moment, I would have. Thankfully, the last call had ended after fifty-eight minutes, which meant Sam hadn't been present for amateur porn hour.

"Why so anxious Ton-Ton? Did something happen that you don't want me to know about?" It was too bad she hadn't had a Kleenex because I'd stuff it in her mouth right now if she had.

I pressed my lips into a firm line, sealing them shut. My mind waged a silent war while I chewed off my lipstick. I could keep my mouth shut and never speak of the incident and also wallow alone in self-pity. Or, I could come clean to the only person I would ever confide in and wallow in shame next to my best friend.

I took in a deep breath and went with option number two. "We had sex." I had to grip my seat for dear life when Sam swerved, nearly colliding with an on-coming car; she'd taken that better than I'd antici-pated. "What the hell, Sam?" My fear and her shock didn't bode well for us surviving the drive home as she veered off the side of the road and onto the dirt.

"Whoa, sorry! He—he didn't force you into it, did he?" Her brows knitted so closely together that they looked more like one furry caterpillar than the two distinct arches that normally resided above her eyes.

My lip trembled first, and then my chin followed close behind it. The anger mixed with concern in her voice was a cocktail I didn't care to drink. *Damn, I wish I had a cocktail.*

"No. It's just...he left right after, Sam. Like he was pulling up his pants as he got out of the limo. He didn't even say goodbye or anything. He just raised his zipper as he closed the door and finished buckling his belt as he walked away—like nothing had happened."

She leaned over the console and gave me a tight hug as the tears streamed down my face. I felt used despite the fact that there had been no insinuation of another outing. And still, I couldn't find it in myself to actually regret how good it felt to have him touch me— for however brief of a period that was. One-night stand or not, it was good. Damn good. And now it was gone.

The more I thought about it, the harder I cried, but Sam never let go. I'd managed to thoroughly soak her shoulder with tears—and possibly a little snot—by the time I finally pulled away. I didn't have a clue how long we'd been there, but two young women on the side of the road late at night did not a rom-com make. This was the start to every bad horror flick ever filmed, and I wasn't interested in starring in *Scream Part Eighty-Four*.

I swiped at my cheeks to dry my tears. "Let's get out of here." I couldn't breathe through my nose, and my voice sounded like I was in a tomb. Couple that with the passing cars, and I was surprised Sam heard me at all.

"Sure. On the way home, let's stop by the store for a huge bucket of ice cream and watch *Comedy Central or* something equally as mindless."

"I thought you were vegan?" Last time I checked, ice cream was made with milk which came from cows, which made it off-limits to my granola sidekick.

Sam rolled her eyes. "I never said I was going to eat it; besides, there are plenty of alternatives that are vegan—and animal—friendly."

I couldn't help but grin. I had to give Sam credit; she was religious about that stuff—never faltered, not even a tiny bit. I couldn't even get her to eat a Peep shaped like an animal. "Are you actually trying to exploit my sadness in an attempt to convert me into a rabbit?"

Sam feigned a stoic facade as she shrugged. "I mean...is it working?" She offered me the cheesiest grin possible, knowing I'd cave because I thought it was cute.

I scoffed. "Fine, but if it tastes like shit, I'm ordering a pizza."

Sam looked like she'd just scratched off a winning lottery ticket and was on her way to cash it in. No one should be that happy over non-dairy ice cream. And when we got to the store, she didn't just get one flavor of tasteless garbage; she bought two. I should have grabbed rice cakes—at least that would have been crunchy and tasteless.

Despite the dairy faux pas, she was still my best friend, who'd stayed up with me all night to keep me from bounding down a depressed hole of slutdom. The whole night was nothing but irresponsible from the paid date to the sex to the lactose-less nightmare and into the morning when I called out of work at the café. I managed to attend classes that afternoon, although I instantly regretted it. It seemed that Jake Hollens was going to haunt me whether I drowned his memory in soy bi-products or faced my depression head-on.

***

"*H*ey, what happened? I didn't see you this morning."

I stared blankly at the guy sitting in front of me,

not bothering to give an answer and hoping he'd take the hint—he did not.

"Um... *Okay?*" Yet, he still didn't give up. "So, what do you think about Hollens Industries; it's pretty epic, right? Their team of lawyers has to be the best in the country if not the world by now. I'd kill to work there. Did you hear they're taking applications for interns?" Travis missed—or possibly ignored—my sigh.

I shrugged and tried to hide my annoyance over a topic involving the family of the only man I wanted to forget. "*Yeah*, defending your boss's sister who disappeared for a year after practically murdering her best friend sounds like the perfect environment to be working in if you ask me."

Travis glared at me with disgust like I'd just spit in his coffee, which was ironic, considering the fact that we worked together in the same run-down café, serving shit-java that I couldn't confirm or deny was free of bodily fluids. "First of all, she wasn't found guilty because she wasn't at fault. *And,* there was nothing other than circumstantial evidence throughout the entire trial to prove otherwise. Mrs. Keller literally just showed us the video. Seriously, Peyton, what's got you so bitchy today?"

I shrugged again. My mood grew fouler as the image of Jake's body kept popping up in my mind. I hadn't paid attention to the video or the lecture. I was lost in my own thoughts, trying to avoid anything Hollens related. My ears perked up—sort of—on the important things that might show up on a test.

"I'm just tired, Travis. Honestly, I'm surprised you're not as cranky as I am, considering you work *doubles* more often than not and cover shifts on the weekends."

He pulled his shoulders back and lifted his chin in pride. "Yeah, well, it's worth it. After we get out of college, the money will go straight to building our own law firm. Wilson & Sanders is going to be the most prestigious firm in the country. Just wait, Peyton." Travis believed every bit of that. He had enough gumption and drive for both of us on the days I struggled.

I couldn't help the upward tilt of my lips. "Yeah, that is something to look forward to."

"Well, whatever it is that's bothering you, I hope you get through it and fast. I can't handle Ashley on my own. She freaks me the fuck out."

I snorted. Our boss was definitely homophobic. When she'd hired Travis, his devasting good looks blinded her. The blue eyes, red hair, freckled face, and slim stature, admittedly, are one of the only reasons why people walked into the cafe. The first time

Travis's boyfriend came in to see him, it was like a flip switched in Ashley's brain.

Now she tended to harass Travis when I wasn't around, preaching to him about his sexuality and how he just needed to *date the right girl.* Ashley was just mad because she couldn't seduce him. Hell, that girl couldn't attract a mosquito much less a gay man.

I had half a mind to tell Travis about the Sugar Daddy app, but his boyfriend definitely wouldn't be okay with his being a paid escort, and after yesterday, I didn't know how I felt about it anymore, either.

Travis and I hadn't known each other for as long as I'd been friends with Sam, but I definitely trusted him when it came to business. Yeah, we're both still learning, but he was like a prodigy. Anyone would be lucky to have his brains on their side, and I'm glad that it was me.

"Don't worry. I'll be fine. I just need some time alone...and some sleep."

He nodded, and thankfully, Mrs. Keller took that moment to dismiss the class.

The rest of the week was just short of torture. Every lecture was more of the same, and no one wanted to pay tuition for someone to teach them about legal cases involving the family of the man who'd ditched them after a good fuck. It was just embarrassing even if there weren't another soul in the classroom who knew my secret. I just about died when another student pulled up an article on their phone. My face was blocked from view—thanks to Jake's broad shoulders—but my silhouette was just as identifiable in my humble opinion.

That's when I realized just how sly that asshole really was. The entire night he'd made sure I wasn't in view from any of the windows. It was surprisingly easy to do, considering he was about a foot and a half taller than me—not really, but he was tall. On the internet, everyone speculated over Mr. Hollens and his *mysterious new girlfriend*. I wished that were the case, but he didn't find me worth the effort of a goodbye much less a second date.

The hits just kept coming. It was the Hollens-family drama all week at school, and then that following weekend, Sam asked me whether or not I planned to continue using the app. I handed over the dollar I'd bet her that night, admitting that she was right. The app was legitimate, and it wasn't the reason behind the decisions I made.

It almost hurt to look at the money Jake had wired to my account. I was even more pissed at the fact that he'd actually had the nerve to include a *tip*. He obviously thought I'd only fucked him for the cash.

Although, if the size of his gratuity indicated his pleasure with my performance, at least I knew I had a backup plan should this whole lawyer gig not work out —legalized prostitution paid well.

Saturday night, I found myself laid out on our couch. I was lucky to attend a private university—and as a senior, I was in the on-campus apartments. Each suite had its own kitchen and bathroom, so no one had to share. And even though the walls weren't sound-proof, it was amazing living on campus and away from the shitty neighborhood I grew up in. This place was expensive, but I worked as much as I could and took out loans to keep the burden from being too much.

I fell asleep for about an hour before the dreams of drowning in sorrow and debt started to consume me. "N-no... M-Money!" I woke myself up with a snort and realized there was a large quantity of drool dripping down my face. "Ugh. Gross." I grunted as I wiped off my jaw with the hem of my sleeve.

That was the only sign I needed to head to bed, but the distance from the living room to my bedroom had me fully awake by the time I laid down again. I yawned when I grabbed my phone from the night-stand. In no time, I'd lost thirty minutes of my life I'd never get back to the stampede of social media and the absurdity of Tik Tok videos. There, between the apps,

Sugar Daddy glowed like a beacon. I pretended I didn't want to open it. I scoffed at the notion of another date. I lied to myself about having no interest. Until the pull was too great, and my finger landed on the button.

I was weak.

So weak.

It had been seven excruciatingly long days since that evening in the limousine, and I'd received no apologies or explanations from Jake—not so much as a poke on the app; and if my sugar daddy couldn't poke me, all hope was lost. This wasn't about finding Mr. Right; it was about finding Mr. Right Now who could pay the freight. There was no need for attachments, just paychecks.

As the weeks went on, I accepted a few more dates. Many of the men were in their late thirties to early forties. They were all kind, and it was safe to say I didn't make another mistake like the one I'd made with Jake. Most of them just needed a companion for a function, and every once in awhile, there was a guy who was just lonely. They weren't after sex, but rather someone to hang out with.

And then came Anthony. I couldn't deny that he'd

been blessed with a solid build, great hair, and a jaw so chiseled it could cut glass. I hadn't asked exactly how old he was, but he was pushing forty—had to be. Despite his age, he still wore his dirty-blond hair in that organized disarray the younger guys did, and his bright eyes varied from light lime to a rich forest green, giving him a youthful vigor. But his clothes contrasted with everything above the neck. Neat and tidy was an understatement, and part of me wondered if he'd made his money in dry cleaning. No one had shirts pressed that perfectly, except Anthony. Somehow, and I couldn't begin to guess how it had come to fruition, Anthony had become an exclusive client of mine.

Knowing his reasoning behind his Sugar Daddy membership and his rather odd appearance, made dating him easier. He was only in this to make another woman jealous. It didn't matter to me in the slightest what his motivation was as long as the chick wasn't some crazy bitch who would maim me in a dark alley. But it didn't take me long to realize, the girl he was after wasn't the least bit interested in Anthony or me. I just didn't have the heart to tell him.

My creep meter probably needed a tune-up or to be refurbished. After Jake, the last thing I should have agreed to was dating in disguise. But when Anthony suggested a short wig and colored contacts the first few times we went out, I just followed his lead. He had crazy amounts of money and blamed the paparazzi and stalkers for the extreme measures. It made sense, *and* I didn't care. He wasn't asking me to put on a rubber suit and suck his toes—although, for the right amount of money, I could have been persuaded—or requesting we role play with him as a baby—I'd draw the line there—and my heart was hurt, so I went with it.

The more time we spent together, the more I learned about the girl he was desperate to woo. Jessica was the love of his life, the reason for my presence at his side, and also a name that sounded terribly familiar. My role as an undercover agent in his mission to make Jessica swoon became one I enjoyed. Going out with a man when neither of you had any interest in the other took all the stress off the table, and Anthony added some amazing pieces to my wardrobe along the way.

At one point, I had asked Anthony why he felt the need to go through all of this hassle for a woman who seemed to be doing her own thing, but he just laughed as if the question were hysterical and preposterous.

His eyes sparkled a rare shade of emerald green that only made an appearance when he talked about her. "For as smart and analytical as Jessica is, she tends to have a gift for being dense about her own feelings."

I leaned back in my chair, instantly irritated by the tone of his voice and the arrogance in his words. They just struck me the wrong way. I glared at him from across the dining table in the small Italian restaurant where we ate. The same place that happened to be this girl's favorite dining establishment. Anthony rolled his eyes and continued speaking, unfazed by my irritation.

"We dropped everything to go on a ten-month trip around Europe. We partied and got lost in the beautiful countries. She'd had a rough time after her best friend died in a car accident. Jessica had been driving.... She continued to blame herself, even though the hearing ruled in her favor."

The tension built within my body, and my muscles began to coil as he spoke. That entire situation sounded eerily similar to the trial Jake's sister was involved in, and the one we'd been studying for weeks in class.

It couldn't possibly be the same person. There was no way in hell that karma had her crosshairs set on me. Six degrees of separation or not, this was too much. I refused to overanalyze it with no way to verify whom he talked about without outing myself—and I'd signed an NDA.

"So, you just wanted to get her mind off things," I

stated, keeping my composure as my mind raced in a million different directions.

Anthony nodded, and I gave him a small smile in return. That was sweet of him. "Of course, she couldn't refuse my charming personality much less this handsome face. I'm irresistible, and she knows it." This was a side of him I'd yet to see. Yes, he'd been confident and on the verge of arrogant, but this just obliterated that fine line he'd danced all around.

He wasn't joking, judging by the look on his face and the tone of his voice. I shook my head, and here I thought the world would have to end before I found someone more self-absorbed than Sam. Now I understood what it meant to appreciate the people around you.

"So, what happened between you two? Did you have a nasty break up?" I didn't really care, but I was curious about what I might have to endure if we came face to face with Jessica in public.

He shifted in his seat, hesitantly as he picked at the food in front of him. "No, our families have been close for years because of our brothers, but she refuses any and all of my advances. I mean, can you believe that? *Me!* All after we had spent a week in the city of romance."

I smirked as I watched his ego deflate like a

balloon. Irritating to humorous. "So, you mean to say that absolutely nothing happened between you two that entire trip?"

Anthony let out a frustrated groan. "It was kind of hard considering her mental state really.... I mean there *was* this one time when things got really emotional for her, and we ended up cuddling on a sofa for about an hour—"

"Well, if she's that comfortable around you, at least you know that you might have a fighting chance with her." *Lies, all lies.*

He gave me a dull look, but my encouraging smile didn't falter. "Of course, I have a chance, that's not the point!" *He didn't have the slightest chance.*

I blinked at him as I registered his words. "You're unbelievable," I muttered under my breath before letting out a snort of disbelief.

He mistook my chortle for humor in her thinking Anthony wasn't as amazing as Anthony believed he was. "The point is, she's ignoring her feelings for me, so I'm just trying to ease them out of her seemingly cold heart."

"And what makes you think she's going to get jealous?"

"The fact that under the influence she said she'd

'fuck me ten times over if she didn't think I'd be smug about it.'"

I raised my brows not able to contain the laughter spilling from my mouth. The entire situation was ridiculous. I just hadn't had any idea how absurd it was until now, but I'd agreed to attend this party where Jessica would be, anyway. Apparently, it was her younger brother's twenty-first birthday.

When the day finally came, I dressed in the outfit Anthony had bought and walked to the nearest park where I'd told him to meet me. I yawned as I waited for him to show and wondered when I'd stop dreaming about Jake. Jake walking away, Jake with other women, Jake beneath me, *Jake, Jake, Jake.* I felt like I'd been dating the man for months, yet the only place I ever saw him was in my dreams—or nightmares.

I had dozed off a few times, sitting at a table on the far side of the park. The sounds of birds, footsteps, and chatter lulled me to sleep as I waited for Anthony's car to arrive. Thankfully, this party was casual, so I hadn't had to wait in a ballgown. It got really awkward standing on a street corner in a ritzy neighborhood in a sequin dress and heels. I snorted awake when Anthony honked the horn; I still didn't understand why the hell I had so much fucking drool coming out of my mouth.

I groaned the second I caught the disgusted look

on Anthony's face. He pointed to the glove compartment, which held a box of tissues.

"Why do you have these in your car?"

"You never know when someone infested with *drool* will step into your *expensive* vehicle. There are Ziploc bags in there, too, so don't even think about dropping those on the floor." The curl of his lip indicated his displeasure, and sadly, it made me happy.

I snorted and saluted. "Yes, *sir*, whatever you say, *sir*."

"Why does that sound like sarcasm?" He honestly appeared perplexed.

I laughed to his dismay. There had to be something in the water that made all the men around me insane.

4

JAKE

A trip that should've lasted a week took a month, and I was already sick and tired of the situation. It was funny at first, but the second my phone was thrown into a fountain due to my sister's inability to keep a firm grasp on any situation, *that* was the last straw.

"I don't know what you're so upset about, Jake. We caught the bitch trying to steal from us, and I got you a new phone with all the data restored."

The data might have been restored, but I still wasn't in the country, and trying to explain my continued silence from across the pond wasn't as easy as it would have been in person—not to mention the time difference. I wasn't really even sure what day it was, much less what time it was in the States—couple that with back-to-back meetings and business dinners, and I couldn't get in a phone call and certainly not a legitimate explanation.

"How are we even related?" I asked, exasperated as I glared at Jessica.

Anyone witnessing our conversation would've thought the situation was hilarious with the kicked puppy look I wore, but I was honestly offended by both her and fate. I'd wired the payment to Peyton's account when I made the donations at the charity gala so I couldn't send her a memo through her account.

I thought of maybe dropping by her house, but she'd mentioned that was her friend's house. She didn't actually live in that neighborhood—they'd just been visiting some chick's parents. I could try to find her through her name alone, but I didn't want her to think I was some kind of creep, especially with all the paparazzi crawling around me like fucking ants these days—they were worse than gnats; they were like a fungus that wouldn't go away.

Never would I have thought I'd be so disappointed to be trapped in beautiful countries like Australia and now France. The food tasted bland unlike the burst of flavor I had experienced the last time I was here, and the colors were duller, as if every hue in the rainbow went straight to the images of that night in the limo. It was cliché and trite, and I didn't give a shit. My world had lit up in the few hours I'd spent with Peyton, and without a way to contact her, it had gone grey and lifeless.

I hadn't dated in years, but that just came with the territory—the rise to the top. Every man my age struggled with the balance of a personal and a professional life. If they didn't find their spouse in college, most never did because after graduation and once Daddy handed over the reins, there was no time for cultivating meaningful relationships with a woman. I was living proof.

Now I just dreamed of a woman I'd met once and wished like hell I was in her bed instead of a hotel five thousand miles away. My imagination had turned Peyton into a dream. It created an image so unattainable, a fantasy I could never reach, and that seemed to pain me even more. Because I could have had her. I just needed five more minutes to get her number and explain what was going on, anything other than sliding my dick back in my pants, raising my zipper, and shutting the door in her face without so much as a goodbye. *Fuck.*

I had no doubts about being with her; I just had to have her in front of me to make it happen. It was all I thought about when we boarded the plane, and the thoughts continued to plague me throughout the flight and back home.

Once we had made it back to the States, all I had wanted to do was find Peyton. But I had already known before I even set foot on domestic soil, there was one engagement after another—today, it just so happened to by my little brother's twenty-first birthday. It was the story of my life and the reason why there was no *Mrs.* Hollens.

"Happy birthday, midget." I smiled, hugging Jamie as I patted a naked baby picture of his onto the back of his shirt. I watched in glee as he proceeded to walk around the party without a care in the world and his tiny little pecker on display for everyone to see.

"You're such an ass." Jessica watched as the guests started to file in.

I noticed Anthony enter, and to my surprise, another woman accompanied him. "Hey." I nudged my twin sister to get her attention. "Who's that girl Anthony brought with him?"

Jessica snapped her head in their direction, and I swore I heard a gasp slip from her mouth.

Strange, for a woman who was adamant about rejecting a man, she sure seemed jealous. When Anthony caught us staring, a devious smirk took over his wide face, and his ugly mug started to head in our direction. But it wasn't him that intrigued me; it was the girl on his arm. All it took was a glimpse of her face —one good look past the heavy makeup—and I'd found the girl who'd plagued my thoughts and wet my dreams for weeks.

I didn't bother with introductions or curbing the attitude behind my question. "What are you doing here with *him?*" Emotions flooded my frontal cortex faster than I could process them—confused, happy, anxious, pissed—mostly fucking pissed. Or maybe hopeful—I didn't think I'd ever see her again.

"Clearly, I'm his plus one, Mr. Hollens." Peyton's tone was sugary sweet as was her smile, but her eyes were daggers, and they pointed directly at me.

Anthony furrowed his brows. "How do you two know each other?"

"Doesn't matter...." I jerked my head toward the bar in the living room. "Hey, Jessica, why don't you and Anthony get some drinks while I talk to Peyton."

Jessica raised her brow at my obvious command, clearly wanting to protest but decided against it. My sister stared at me in disbelief before giving me a glare that indicated I owed her more than an explanation for this favor. She didn't say a word as she dragged Anthony by the elbow to the nearest watering hole.

Outside of Anthony's initial confusion, he hadn't

seemed the least bit put off or perturbed by being escorted away from his "date." There wasn't even a moment's hesitation or an ounce of protest. If anything, he'd appeared anxious to join Jessica, and it wouldn't have mattered if I'd sent her to the bar or the bathroom.

I led Peyton into an empty hallway, away from all the prying ears and eyes. She followed me reluctantly and without a word.

"What do you want, Jake?" The venom in her voice took me by surprise, although it probably shouldn't have. Even under the veil of a whisper, she failed to disguise her unhappiness.

"After what happened between us, I thought—"

"*What?* That you could just walk away without saying anything for *weeks* and think I'd be waiting and willing for you to return?" She hissed at me, but I appreciated her ability to keep her voice down.

"No, I—"

"Not to mention, you're here with someone else. So why do you care who I showed up with? Just wondering who the next guy on the list would be? Wonder how much he pays to get in my pants?" She crossed her toned arms and cocked out her hip. Despite her tough posture, her lip trembled as she fought off tears. "I'm not a whore, Jake." No truer words had ever been spoken; I could see it in her eyes —I'd been the exception.

I furrowed my brows as the feeling of disgust flowed through me. Not once had I thought of her that way. And for the love of all things holy, how could she possibly have mistaken Jessica for my girlfriend? *Gross.*

"No, of course not." I raked my hand through my hair and blew out an exaggerated breath. "And Jessica's my—"

She held up her hand, stopping me. "Don't."

I tried not to smirk at the blush that rose on her cheeks but ultimately failed, and she easily redirected her glare back to me. So, I tried a different approach. "I'm sorry for leaving the way I did. I only had five minutes to get on the plane. I didn't want to ditch you like that, but it was important." It was vague, but now wasn't the time to divulge the details. Hell, I was lucky I'd managed to get the time with her to apologize at all.

She raised a brow and pursed her lips together tightly, not entirely convinced.

"I just got back from Australia and then France. It was a seventeen-hour flight, non-stop meetings, and then we went to France. I've been gone on business since that night, Peyton. My phone ended up in a fountain, and by the time I got a new one..." I pulled my hair in frustration and took a deep breath. "It's not quite as easy for an American to get a new phone in Europe."

Peyton shifted in her stance as her posture became a little less hostile and rigid. She remained silent, and I could tell that she was still perfectly content to stay angry. I grabbed her hand, and as much as she looked like she wanted to pull away and possibly smack me across the face, she maintained eye contact and didn't move to throw a punch. There was a magnetic force that drew the two of us together. I'd felt it the night we met, and it was just as strong now. I couldn't stop myself, not that I wanted to.

I leaned in slowly, giving her the chance to refuse me, to push me away. She did neither as I pressed my lips to hers. It was electric and gratifying, and it was also interrupted by footsteps coming down the hall. Peyton pushed me away, ending the excruciatingly short kiss.

"What—" I began, but she shook her head, stopping me in my tracks.

She stepped away and headed back toward the door, but I grabbed her wrist, stopping her. "I can't do this." Tears welled in her eyes, and I wanted nothing more than to wipe them away, but that wouldn't happen today—she wouldn't let it.

"Wait." I pulled out a pen from my back pocket

and wrote my number on her wrist where her sleeve easily hid it. My eyes met hers, and I hoped she saw my sincerity. "Please, just, call me when you have a chance. I don't want this to be the last time we see each other."

Again, she remained silent as her eyes narrowed a bit more, glanced down at the numbers I'd inked on her skin, and then Peyton shook her head. She offered me a weary smile that I couldn't read, but it was a smile, nonetheless. And then she walked back toward the foyer.

That was all I needed to lift my mood—just the possibility of more time with Peyton. I turned in the direction of the footsteps I'd heard and found Jamie waiting for my attention with a picture held up in his hand.

"What the fuck is this?"

I laughed before getting my ass out of there. Jamie chased after me, hot on my trail. It wouldn't matter how old either of us got, he'd always be my little brother, and I'd do everything in my power to fuck with him well into old age.

"Get back here, asshole. This isn't funny. Putting my baby cheeks on display for everyone to see like that, what kind of older brother are you?" It wasn't the butt cheeks he needed to be upset about.

By the time our chase was over and we headed back into the main room, gasping for air, I noticed that Peyton was nowhere to be found, although Jessica and Anthony seemed to be having a good time, chatting. I asked where Peyton was, but Anthony said she'd taken a cab home. I wanted to slap him upside his inconsiderate head, but I thought it better to let it go.

wo weeks passed without a word from Peyton, and I'd started to get restless. She was keeping her distance. She still thought I was an asshole. But that wasn't a game I was going to let her play. Peyton didn't get to decide our fate without a little interference. I hadn't wanted to contact her through the Sugar Daddy app again. I wanted to spend time with her because she wanted to be there, not because I paid her. But I wasn't above doing what had to be done to get my second chance, even if that meant making her an offer for a date she couldn't refuse.

I opened the app—grateful she hadn't thought to block me—and filled in the details of my proposal. It felt a bit *Pretty Woman*-ish, but I had money, and I wasn't ashamed to buy her time. Both occasions I'd been in her presence, the electric pull, the magnetic connection was so strong that I was certain if I could get her alone for a weekend, I'd convince her to see things my way. And I attached a hefty dollar figure to sweeten the proposition.

I'd no sooner submitted the deal to her account than a message popped up. I wasn't even aware the app had a messenger, but when I clicked on the notification, sure enough, there it was.

Peyton: Are you insane?

Me: I want to make sure you don't say no.

Peyton: Why are you doing this?

Me: To have a chance to explain.

Peyton: Explain what?

Me: What happened.

Peyton: You've done that already.

Me: Okay, then I want a second chance.

Peyton: For what?

Me: Are we going to keep going in circles?

Peyton: Until you answer my question.

Me: I've answered them all.

Peyton: What do you want, Jake?"

Me: A weekend. Just one. Friday-Sunday. You and me with no interruptions or distractions. And if you don't want to talk to me at the end of that, I'll leave you alone.

There was a long bout of silence, and no little bubbles danced on the screen to indicate she was typing. Either she was considering the offer, or she'd signed out, and I wouldn't hear from her again. Since she hadn't rejected the date online, I held my breath and my hope.

The light went green. My submission moved from pending to accepted. And then came the bubbles.

Peyton: One shot, Mr. Hollens.

One shot was all I needed. By the end of this weekend, Peyton would never want to leave my side, and I'd do my best to convince her not to.

I picked up Peyton at a bookstore that I assumed was close to where she lived. It was near the college I'd attended, and a lot of student housing was nearby. She wasn't comfortable telling me where she lived and based on our history thus far, I understood that—even if I didn't care for it.

The moment I saw her, my heart stopped just like it had the night of the gala. Except for today, she was all Peyton. A flowy, sheer top that I could see through to a spaghetti strap, fitted tank beneath, skinny jeans, and boots with heels. Her hair was long and loose, and the only bits of makeup I could confirm were mascara and lip gloss. She was confident in a way she hadn't been in the evening attire, and I instantly decided I liked this version of her better.

I leaned in to kiss her cheek, and a soft blush rose on her skin. "Hey, gorgeous."

She didn't have anything with her other than a backpack, but I took it and slung it over my shoulder. Peyton smiled, but it was shy, sweet almost. It dawned on me that she was nervous. The night we'd gone out before she'd been quirky yet confident. Peyton also knew there was a time limit on how long she would be with me that evening. She's committed to an entire weekend at my beck and call, and her doubt was written all over her body.

There was nothing I would love more than to put her in the back of a limo and ease away all the stress and hesitation that had her fingers twisted together and her grey eyes weary. But that wasn't on the evening's agenda, at least not unless Peyton decided to change the plans.

I took her hand, and the warmth of her skin against mine ignited something deep within me, and it wasn't just the twitch in my pants. There was more, so much more than just a beautiful face. Most women would have put aside their hurt in favor of a chance at having their names added to my bank accounts, but not this one. Her pride and self-worth were worth more than anything I could offer monetarily. She wasn't *playing* hard to get; she *was* hard to get.

I clicked the remote to unlock the doors, and Peyton glanced around. Clearly, she wasn't expecting the Aston Martin, but I wanted into this woman's heart, and there was no better way to start that journey than in the Vanquish. Her little gasp alerted me to her parted lips, and damn if I didn't want to kiss them.

"This is beautiful." She wasn't wrong.

I opened the door and set her backpack on the floor before stepping back to allow her to sit. "Your chariot awaits."

Peyton slid by me and onto the buttery-soft, black leather. "Where's your driver?"

"Wilton? I believe he's at a dance recital for his granddaughter." I winked and closed the door. I didn't stare at her as I rounded the hood, but I saw her head follow me, and those perfect, pouty lips were still parted when I opened the driver's door.

She cleared the surprise from her expression by the time I started the ignition. "Do you know how to drive this thing?" Her tone was playful, but there was an element of doubt laced in the words.

I put the car in gear and glanced over my shoulder before pulling away from the curb. "I've been behind the wheel once or twice since I got my license."

"I figured you had people for that." Her comment stung, even whispered under her breath.

I could have defended myself, but I deserved whatever she dished out. I'd hurt her, and it appeared now was the time for her to reciprocate. I just hoped that it wouldn't take long for her to see that the person she believed me to be wasn't who I was at all. The version of me that makes it into the public eye, is not the me I am behind closed doors. Very few people, especially women, ever see this me. It makes me vulnerable, and weakness is like blood in shark-infested waters. It attracts predators.

I worked my way through the gears as we headed out of the city and toward my house. Peyton sat silently in the seat next to me, just taking in the scenery. Her expression softened when the traffic died down and the ocean came into sight. There were virtually no cars on the cliffside road that snaked along the coast, and being in the passenger seat gave her a totally unobstructed view. It was breathtaking. I snuck peeks at her as I took the corners; the car hugged the turns with engineered ease. The grace and agility of this machine were matched by no other. I loved driving it almost as much as I enjoyed watching her relax and let go.

"Oh my God." She turned in excitement to glance at me and then pointed toward the water. "Dolphins." Peyton's face had lit up like a Christmas tree, and it was more beautiful than the view.

I couldn't focus on the scenery if I planned to keep the car between the white lines, but her happiness made my chest swell.

"There are tons of them."

I wasn't surprised. We were high enough up that

she could likely see a couple of miles off the coast, and the area was known for dolphins. They loved to play, and this was an area they were left undisturbed. "Do you spend a lot of time at the beach?"

She shook her head and glanced over her shoulder again, but returned her focus to the water when she started to talk. "Between work, classes, and homework, I don't have a lot of time to play these days."

"Are you still working at the café?"

Peyton slumped into the seat and turned her entire body my direction. "You remember that?"

Without taking my eyes off the highway, I reached over and took her hand. "I remember everything you said."

Peyton didn't pull away or turn to look out the window. Instead, she twined her fingers with mine. "So, what are your plans for us this weekend?" There was no sass in her tone or expectation, just intrigue.

I rubbed my thumb over her skin and hoped she was down with low key. I had been serious when I said no interruptions or distractions. My weekend was going to be all about her. There were parts of my life that no one got to see, and those were the things I wanted to share with Peyton in hopes that she would open up, as well.

"Honestly, not a lot. I thought you'd enjoy the

scenic route to my house—and dinner on the patio when we get there. I got a nice bottle of wine for us, and I just want to spend time getting to know you."

"Do you live far from here?"

I chuckled. "I live about twenty minutes from the bookstore." I watched as her brow scrunched in confusion. "But since we aren't in a hurry to get anywhere, I wanted to enjoy the ride."

Her eyes sparkled in the waning sun, and I wished I could grab the back of her neck and haul her across the car. My lips ached to touch hers, and my tongue wanted to do more than delve into her mouth to explore. But all good things come to those who wait, and I had patience in spades.

"So where do you live, Mr. Hollens? Are we leaving the state? Should I have Sam on tracker?" Peyton's lips twitched in humor.

We'd gone an incredibly circular route to reach my house, but her question came at the perfect time. As we left the highway and veered down what appeared to be a desolate road, I lifted my hand to indicate she could see for herself. The gates opened as I pulled up, and I took the winding driveway to the circular pad. As much as I wasn't trying to amaze her with wealth, Peyton didn't disguise her wonder as she took in my home.

"This is...wow. You live here alone?" She opened the door and started to get out before I'd even taken off my seatbelt.

I followed her out of the car, and when I reached her side, she stopped to turn in a circle.

"You have a fountain in your driveway that's bigger than the swimming pool at my apartment complex." Peyton continued to turn where she stood. "Are those horses?" She didn't wait for me to nod when she completed her circle and stared straight up. "Holy crap."

This was totally unproductive and not helping me show Peyton that I could do normal. Not that I had any idea what normal really was. I just needed her to know that our lives didn't have to be dictated by other people, and that what had happened that first night with the plane was a fluke, not my every day. My time at the office might not belong to me, but I'd make sure that every second outside of it listed Peyton as a top priority.

"Come on. Let's go inside." I took her backpack from her hand, and she followed a couple of steps behind me.

No sooner had I reached out to open the door than Gwen greeted us. "Good evening, Mr. Hollens." She took the bag from my hand and smiled warmly at

Peyton. "I take it you've had a nice day?" Her gaze came back to me, and she lifted her brows in suggestion.

Gwen had been with my parents for as long as I could remember. She might as well be my grand-mother. I loved her like one.

I kissed her cheek and then commenced with introductions. "Gwen, this is Peyton. Peyton, this is Gwen."

"I've heard quite a bit about you, Peyton. It's a pleasure to meet you." Gwen bowed her head just slightly and crossed her hands in front of her.

Peyton peeked at me and then met Gwen's gaze. "It's nice to meet you, as well."

Gwen set Peyton's backpack next to the door once we were all inside. "I'm just getting ready to leave for the weekend. Are you sure you don't need anything before I go?"

I shook my head. "I'm good." But I knew she couldn't let it go with that. "I promise. If I need you, or if I set the house on fire, I'll call."

She patted my cheek and looked back to Peyton as she did it. "Such a good boy."

Kill me now. Peyton giggled next to me.

Just before Gwen slipped out the door, she lifted her hand to cup Peyton's cheek. "If he does anything stupid, my number is on the fridge. You call me." Gwen stroked Peyton's cheekbone, and something passed between them that had to be understanding.

Peyton nodded quickly with a bright smile. Yep, they were already conspiring against me, but hopefully, Peyton's instant love for Gwen would win brownie points for me. Which made me think, if she ever tasted Gwen's brownies, the two of us would be exchanging vows in no time.

The door closed with us inside and Gwen out, and Peyton stepped close to me. Her hand settled on my hip, and her neck craned. The second her front pressed to my side, I had to bite my cheek to keep still.

"I like her." Mischief glimmered in her eyes, and if I didn't know better, I'd say they'd been making deals with the devil behind my back.

"Most people do. I'd be lost without her."

Something in those few words left Peyton as putty in my hands, but I didn't know what. She lifted onto the balls of her feet and pressed a kiss to my jaw. I wrapped my arm around her waist and squeezed her to me. Then I took the chance of dipping my head, and thankfully, she turned in to meet my lips. It was brief, and I definitely wanted more. Standing in the foyer probably wasn't the best place to make that happen, especially not this soon after picking her up.

"How do you know her?"

I let Peyton go to move inside the house. The entrance was nice, but it certainly wasn't my favorite spot to have a conversation. "I stole her from my parents' staff when I got out of college."

Her jaw dropped. "She works for you?"

"What else would she be doing here?" I wasn't sure I wanted to know what Peyton thought I was doing with a *much* older woman in my house.

She shrugged. "I don't know. What does she do?"

"Until I get married, she runs my house. She is responsible for the staff, the routines, the maintenance, my schedule." I opened the fridge and started to pull out the stuff I'd bought to make dinner. "And basically, she keeps me in line."

Peyton leaned against the marble island, watching me. "A live-in secretary?"

I slammed the refrigerator door closed and rushed to push Peyton behind my back while I quickly glanced around the corner and toward the front entry. "Phew." I turned back to her with a smirk. "Don't ever let Gwen hear you say that."

Peyton giggled at my theatrics. "That she lives here or that she's your secretary?"

I turned back toward the food I'd laid out. "Either. Gwen doesn't live here, although she might as well.

And she's more like my guardian angel than any kind of admin. I remember her being around when I was potty training."

Peyton's brows shot up. "Either you have a great memory, or you were a late bloomer."

I glared at her playfully. "We don't talk about that time in my life. It was difficult for everyone."

She shook her head, but her grin told me she got my pathetic attempt at humor. "Moving on." Her stomach growled loudly enough to echo in the kitchen, bouncing off the high ceilings. Her cheeks blushed with embarrassment, but I thought it was cute.

"Hungry?"

"I didn't have time to eat today. I had an early shift at the café this morning and classes this afternoon." The sheepish look on her face bothered me. Lots of college kids ate like crap and just as many had menial jobs to get by, but I wanted better for Peyton.

She deserved better.

I could give it to her if she'd let me, but now wasn't the time for that conversation. "Please tell me you're not a vegetarian."

Her perfect nose scrunched up and her brow went down. "Umm no. I believe in the food chain. My room-mate, however, is a different story. We have this battle on a daily basis."

"Good. Me, too. I believe animals were put on this earth for a reason, and that was for me to eat them." I gathered the steaks that I'd started marinating that morning along with the bowl of vegetables I planned to grill. "Can you grab two wine glasses," I pointed to the cabinet, "and the wine." I nodded to the bottle on the counter.

I stood in awe as she lifted onto her toes to grab the glasses, and I didn't miss that she glanced back at the bottle over her shoulder before she correctly chose the appropriate stemware. My girl was good. It might not matter to most people, but in my world, that was the type of detail that gave people away. And while I didn't care if she wanted to drink red or white out of a mason jar or a bowl, that wasn't true of the company I kept for business dealings. If Peyton were going to be mine, I wanted her at my side every time she could be there. Unfortunately, that would include dinners with clients and charity events. It was good to know, I wouldn't have to worry about her being under a micro-scope and the sneers people would make behind her back about her etiquette and upbringing.

With Peyton on my heels, I made my way through the kitchen and to the French doors that lead to the patio. I pushed down the handle with my elbow and eased it open. She followed, and her eyes went wide when she saw the back of the house. The gardens were pretty and well-cared for, but I was quite certain it was the pool—and the hot tub that heated it—that caught her attention. She closed her mouth and made it to the table without stumbling on the cobblestone.

I set the plate of meat and bowl of vegetables on the wrought iron table. "Want a tour?"

Her hair blew with the light breeze, and she pulled a thick strand from her lips. Peyton didn't speak; she just nodded. My heart leaped at the sight of her innocence. How she'd ended up on that damn app, I'd never know, but she was lucky she hadn't been eaten alive.

"Let me start the grill, and it can heat up while we walk."

"You're going to make dinner?" She nearly choked on her words.

I lit the burners and closed the lid. "Yeah. Who did you think was going to cook?"

She shrugged. "Your chef? I don't know."

I dropped my head back as laughter barreled from my chest and out my mouth. "Sweetheart, no one cooks around here but me. Unless you count Gwen's baking brownies." I slid my arm around her waist and pulled her to me, kissing her forehead when she landed against my chest. "I don't bake."

She peered up at me, and I decided that was my favorite way to see her—flush with me. Her grey irises had returned to a sultry blue color only inches away, and her perfect mouth begged to be kissed. "You cook?"

"Yeah, babe. I cook. I mean I'm not going to be awarded a Michelin star or anything, but I get by. Although I have to admit, I don't usually have time to do my own grocery shopping. But Gwen doesn't do that, either. I have it delivered."

Peyton rolled her eyes, but I could tell that the idea of my doing things for myself appealed to her. I didn't give her a chance to comment before I pulled her off the patio and down the steps. Pathways scoured the property, winding through the enormous gardens once we'd passed the pool.

She stopped to touch the flowers, but they weren't any of the ones most women would. Peyton wasn't attracted to the roses or the tulips. It was the fields of wildflowers that weren't actually part of my gardens that she found fascinating. "Can I pick one?"

"It's illegal in forty-eight of the fifty states, but I won't tell anyone."

Peyton jerked her hand back, leaving the bloom intact. So, I chose one for her, plucked it, and tucked it behind her ear. My hand lingered on her jaw, and I couldn't stop myself from tipping her head back. I gave her ample time to push me away, tell me no, stop me—she did none of those. In fact, she welcomed my kiss and parted her lips. My tongue found hers, and there at the back of my property, we shared a kiss more intimate than sex. The shell she'd hardened around her heart cracked under the heat of our exchange. And when we finally broke apart, I knew Peyton had opened the door to giving me a second chance.

"How does a single guy end up with more flowers than the botanical gardens?"

We made our way back toward the house. As long as we'd been gone, I'd be lucky if I hadn't burned the house down.

"My mom loved flowers. She had a heavy hand in it before she passed away. After that, I think I kept them going because they remind me of her. There were probably half as many when she died as there are now."

Peyton took my hand and turned her head up to me as we walked. "Do you spend a lot of time out here?"

"More than you'd probably expect."

She didn't pry, which I appreciated, but it was a chance to give her a piece of understanding that she might not receive otherwise.

"Her death is why my dad is the way he is."

Peyton didn't even pause. She kept strolling through the myriad of colors, enjoying the open blooms. "How so?"

"They had a fairytale romance. High school sweethearts. When she was diagnosed with cancer, he thought she would beat it. But it was too advanced. She died less than four weeks later, and he lost his mind with grief. You now see the end result."

"I'm sorry to hear that." The sympathy in her tone was likely more for me than my father. "I don't think that gives him the right to be cruel to people, but I can't imagine what that kind of loss would be like."

I squeezed her hand. "He's not the easiest man to get along with, but he'll come around." I didn't know why I was trying to convince her of my dad's worth. At this point, I wasn't sure I'd see her past Sunday. I certainly didn't need to sell her on my family.

She pulled me along the path as we neared the pool. "Now that you've wowed me with your flora and fauna, I need you to showcase your grilling skills. I'm starving, and you promised me a steak." Peyton had a natural ability to lead me where she wanted to go and away from topics she wasn't interested in discussing.

We spent the next few hours relaxing by the pool with full bellies, sipping wine. As the sun dipped below the horizon, the lights and fountain in the pool came on. The white noise created a perfect musical backdrop for the evening. It was getting late, and Peyton looked exhausted. If I went by the number of yawns I'd seen come from her mouth, she was ready for bed an hour ago.

I stood and began to gather the glasses and the empty wine bottles from the table. Leaning back in her chair, she stared up at me. God, she was gorgeous. I bent at the waist, pressing my lips to her forehead. I wanted more—so much more—but I restrained my desire to take her on the porch. She believed I'd used her that night we'd met, and the next time it happened, it had to be because she wanted it, not because I pursued it. Peyton had wanted it that night, but I had blown her trust when I had left.

"I'll be right back."

I took the glasses inside and put them in the dish-washer, and then I tossed the bottles into the recycling bin. It took me a minute to regain my composure, adjust myself in my pants, and rejoin her on the porch. Peyton watched my approach with hooded eyes. I wondered if she fought the same urges I did.

"You ready to call it a night?" God, I wanted her in my bed. The thought of having her down the hall instead of next to me was excruciating, but I'd made up my mind when she agreed to stay that I wouldn't push her.

She nodded and yawned. "I need my backpack."

We grabbed it on our way to the stairs. Peyton walked quietly beside me. I couldn't sense any apprehension coming off her, making me rethink putting her in a guest room. But I decided to stay the course. I passed the room I intended to put her in to show her where I would be, in case she needed anything.

My door stood open, and I reached inside to turn on a light. "This is my room." I flipped the switch, bathing the room again in darkness just before she stepped inside. "Your room is down here." Our steps now seemed ominous on the marbled floors, and Peyton definitely appeared surprised.

This was my favorite of all the guest rooms, although I'd never let anyone else stay in it. I didn't have a lot of overnight visitors, and the only ones of the female persuasion were all related to me. I reached around the corner to illuminate the space. She gasped when it came into full view.

I wished I could say I had designed the space or picked out the furniture. I hadn't, but I had hired the interior designer who seemed to get my style like he was in my head. I had no idea when he'd designed the room that Peyton would be the one this room had been created for, but now it almost seemed like destiny—except for the fact that I wanted her in my room and not the next room over.

"It's beautiful." She homed in on the water feature across from the bed. "Is that a waterfall?"

"It's supposed to help you sleep." It made sense when Blane explained it during the decorating process, so I went with it. "You can adjust the temperature of the room and the lighting." I pointed to the discreet panel on the wall. "And there's a remote in the night-stand if you don't want to get up." I proceeded into the room to point out the bathroom, which was stocked with anything and everything she could ever need—at least, that's what Jessica told me when I'd called her over here last night to make sure I hadn't missed anything.

Peyton licked her lips and stared at me, confused. I didn't want to play games, but I'd accomplished exactly what I'd set out to. There was no doubt in my mind that she'd believed part of her weekend with me would include taking off her clothes. I delighted in knowing I'd thrown her off, kept her on her toes.

"Do you need anything before I go to bed?" I studied her dazed expression, although I kept my mouth shut. If I said much more, I'd beg her to follow me back down the hall.

She shook her head and then closed the space between us. Her warm hands pressed against my chest when she lifted onto her toes to press a chaste kiss to my lips. "Thank you. I had a really nice evening."

A really nice evening. Not the words I wanted to hear out of her mouth. I'd prefer to hear her scream my name as I brought her to orgasm or chant to a higher power as she begged for release. But that would have to do. For now.

"Goodnight, Peyton."

Her fingers clutched mine until I couldn't walk any farther without letting them go. There was something akin to disappointment in her expression, but her desire would only grow if I didn't readily offer myself to her. So I went to my room, then the bathroom, and I turned on the shower. As soon as I got under the spray, I let my mind drift to a naked Peyton in my lap, riding my cock, praising my name, as pleasure took us both. And when I exploded onto the shower floor, I cringed as I realized it hadn't provided any relief. I still needed her. I still wanted her. Only now, I knew she was down the hall, and I couldn't have her.

PEYTON

The sunlight poured through the windows. I blinked the sleep from my eyes, wishing I'd closed the drapes before I'd gotten into the huge, soft, cloud of a bed. I'd been so blown away by Jake having gone to sleep in his own room, that I'd been in a stupor when I went to the bathroom to get ready for bed.

There, on the counter, I'd found a beautiful, pale-blue box tied with a white, satin ribbon. The card attached had my name on it, yet nothing else. Clearly, it was from Jake, but I had no idea why he'd left it on the vanity. I'd untied the ribbon, lifted the lid, and then carefully unfolded the gold tissue paper. Inside was the most elegant, sensual, sexy, and expensive nightgown I'd ever seen much less touched. The silk was unlike anything I'd ever felt, and the white was more pristine than snow. With intricate lace that lined the hems and tiny straps, it was nearly weightless, and holy hell, when I slipped it over my head and onto my bare skin, I nearly orgasmed standing there.

I fought traipsing down the hall in my new nightie to thank Jake, thinking it was all the wine the two of us had shared. I'd gotten really good at lying to myself about my feelings for the man. But now, in the light of the morning, that same silk tickled my skin, and I was sober as a nun. I'd fought my urge for Jake for weeks, and last night, he'd been the perfect gentleman. This morning, I wasn't feeling quite so restrained, and I prayed like hell that he was still in his room. There was no way I'd go roaming through his house in search of him in this slip of a gown.

I eased out of bed, hating to leave the comfort behind and went to the bathroom. I brushed my teeth —nobody wanted morning breath involved in seduction—and then combed my hair. Again, I admired the nightie in the mirror, turning this way and that to see the plunging back. I licked my lips and pinched my cheeks for a bit of color and headed to the bedroom door. I opened it quietly and stuck out my head, looking both ways for oncoming traffic. Once I'd determined it was safe and I wasn't in danger of being seen by any of Jake's staff—not that I'd seen anyone here other than Gwen—I stepped out of my room with all the confidence in the world.

That was—until I reached his door. And then I stood there like an idiot. It wasn't closed completely, but I felt weird trying to peek through the crack to see if Jake was inside. Finally, I took a deep breath, straightened my spine, and pulled back my shoulders. He hadn't brought me here this weekend to reject me. In fact, the idea that he hadn't wanted to sleep with me last night plagued me until sleep finally took me under...and I realized he was giving me space.

I was done with space. I wanted a connection. And now, I had to make it.

The heavy wood door didn't make a sound as I eased it open, and neither did my bare feet as I padded across the room. Clearly, I did not have what it took to be a ninja because I hadn't even reached his bed when Jake rolled onto his back, and his face continued my direction. Sleepily, his lids parted, and I'd never seen anything as sexy in my life.

"Hey, beautiful." He held out his hand for me. "Did you sleep well?"

I licked my lips and nodded before I finally eked out a reply. "I did." My fingers laced through his, and Jake pulled me the rest of the way. I fell onto the bed, and he managed to roll me into him so that my side was flush with his. "Although it was a little cold."

Jake brushed the hair from my face and kissed my temple. "You should have adjusted the temperature in the room." He'd missed the insinuation.

"Oh, it wasn't that."

He snuggled closer to me and pulled the blanket on top of both of us. "You should have come to get me. I would have fixed it."

I traced circles with the tips of my fingers over the smattering of hair on his chest. "Or maybe you should have just stayed." I sucked at playing coy, but that had gotten his attention.

"You didn't invite me to stay. It's your house. I'm your guest. Isn't it you who should have invited me to stay?" I pulled back and raised my brows for him to see the suggestion.

And see it he did. "I'm not very good at playing host. I've never had a woman spend the night in my house." He shifted and lifted himself onto his elbow, and I struggled to keep my lips closed and the shock from my face at that proclamation. "I wasn't sure of the protocol."

I didn't have a snappy comeback, so I went with gracious instead. "Thank you for the nightgown."

"It looks beautiful on you." His lips met mine. "But Peyton..."

"Mmm?" I couldn't form words when we were this close, when I wanted so much—of him.

He kissed me again, this time with the slip of his tongue, teasing me. "You'd look even better out of it." Jake slid his fingers down my arm with a featherlight touch.

Chills raced over my skin, and heat pooled between my legs. I didn't want to wait to see what he did, yet I wasn't interested in being the aggressor, either. We'd done fast and reckless in the limo. I wanted to see what Jake could do when he took his time, or rather *what* he would do when he had all the time in the world.

He didn't disappoint. Jake's lips and kisses and soft caresses explored every exposed inch of my body. He didn't race to get me out of the nightgown; instead, he worked around it, over it, under it. Teasing, tasting, tempting. And when I thought I couldn't take any more of the foreplay, Jake settled his hips between my thighs, keeping his weight on his forearms at my sides, and took my mouth to show me what he intended to do next. His tongue delved and tangled with mine. Electricity shot straight to my core. My back arched into his chest. Heat radiated off his tanned, toned skin, yet when I reached for the waistband of his boxers, he captured my hand and then held both of my wrists above my head.

"Don't move." It wasn't really a command so much as a plea, and the hunger in his eyes was all I needed to stay put.

Jake shimmied down my body and rocked back onto his calves. I watched without moving as he worked the gown up my sides, then I lifted my ass to help him, then my spine, and finally up just enough for him to drag the material over my head. Then I resumed my position. Jake stood to drop his underwear to the floor along with the white silk he'd tossed there. His dick stood thick and proud, and my mouth watered at the sight. But Jake didn't give me time to admire his masculine form. He slipped back onto the mattress and nestled himself between my legs.

His tongue snaked out, coating his lips with moisture. Part of me wanted to kiss those lips as he sank deep inside me, and another part of me wanted to watch him do it. As he laid down on top of me, Jake made the decision to have the first and not the last. His dick slid between my folds, coated in my heat. The head bumped my clit and drove me mad with lust when he withdrew. He knew what he was doing, and he'd laid down to ensure I couldn't use my hands to assist.

"Please..." I moaned the word as much as I said it.

He nudged my ear with his nose and whispered a warm breath onto the skin behind my ear. "Please, what?"

I might not be able to move my hands, but I could certainly use my feet. I dug my heels into his ass cheeks to encourage his hips forward.

Jake chuckled. He also didn't give me what I wanted. "Tell me what you need, sweetheart."

I swore men got off on this kind of shit, and for the first time in my life, I finally understood why. I was a panting, writhing mess of desperation under his touch. It had to be huge for the ego. "You."

He poised his head at my entrance and tilted his hips forward just enough for me to feel him there, although he still didn't give me what I wanted. "This?"

The next time I used my legs to my advantage, he didn't stop himself from sinking deep into my warmth, all the way to the hilt. It took me a second to catch my breath, and he gave me the time to adjust. Once he did, the waves of pleasure rolled in along with the supple motion of his hips. It was better than I remembered it the first time, and that had been fucking amazing.

He finally released my wrists and let my hands

roam free. One cupped his jaw, the other grabbed his neck, I couldn't get close enough to him, even though there wasn't space between us. As we climbed toward that peak together, I wanted more. I became desperate for it. But it wasn't just the orgasm I chased; it was Jake.

And when I exploded around him, I realized I wanted it all.

After Jake gave me one of the most memorable orgasms of my life, he then proceeded to eat me for breakfast. It was after noon by the time we finally got out of bed, and that only happened because my stomach ratted me out. I could no longer deny being hungry since it wouldn't stop rumbling. I would have starved to death if Jake had let me continue to indulge on his body and the ecstasy he offered. Unfortunately, he needed sustenance to keep going.

Lunch had led us back outside to the spot we'd enjoyed last night, and the pool called my name.

"We can get in if you want, Peyton." He'd seen me eyeing the water.

It wasn't overly hot, but the hot tub that cascaded into the pool looked like it would be refreshing regardless of the temperature outside. The rockwork surrounding both, coupled with the gardens, made this feel like an oasis.

"I didn't bring a swimsuit."

He used his foot to push the edge of my chair out so that my knees faced his. Jake leaned forward, snatched my hand, and pulled me into his lap. "Since when do you need a swimsuit to get into a pool?"

I felt the heat of a blush rise on my cheeks. "You might be comfortable with your staff seeing us both naked, but *I* am not."

"Baby, my staff has weekends off. Gwen locked the front gates behind her. Even if someone wanted or needed to come by unexpectedly, they'd have to stop to be buzzed in. And if you haven't noticed, I'm not the least bit interested in buzzing anyone in." He lifted his brows and waited for another excuse to come out of my mouth.

I didn't have one. That was it. If there were no chance of us being caught by the gardener, then I was absolutely down with skinny dipping in Jake's fabulous pool. I didn't wait for him to extend another invitation. I stood, unbuttoned my shorts, shimmied them and my panties down my legs, and then I stripped off my tank top and bra. Naked as the day was long, I waited for Jake to get with the program. When he seemed content just to watch, I shrugged, took two giant steps toward the edge of the water, and then dove in.

To say it was invigorating was an understatement. When I surfaced, my breasts were like buoys on top of the water, and it took less time for Jake to undress and join me than it had for me to dive in.

Before the day was over, he'd fucked me seven ways from Sunday all over the pool, the deck, the hot tub, and anywhere else he could find a spot to take me. And I had let him without reservation. It wasn't just sex—yes, it was incredible—there was a connection there. Every time the two of us became one, another piece of me became his. Neither one of us even had to get off; it was just being joined together that we both craved—the orgasms were a bonus. And there were a bunch of them.

I laid on a lounge chair with my back facing what remained of the sun. "I could do this every day. I don't know how you ever get anything done." My eyes were closed, and it wasn't until the words were out of my mouth that I realized what I'd said. Instead of making things worse by backtracking about *doing this every day*, I kept my mouth shut.

"I'd love to have you here every day doing just this."

I waited for a but, yet one didn't come. "Living in the lap of luxury."

He took my hand and brought it to his lips, kissing my knuckles. "You deserve the best life has to offer, Peyton. I wish you'd let me give it to you."

I didn't probe into what he meant. It didn't matter. I wasn't looking for a white knight to rescue me. My plans included doing that for myself, and I was well on my way. "I'd love for you to give me something else."

He lifted his head, his eyes wide with wonder. "Name it."

I leaned as close to him as I could without lifting myself off the chair or dumping the lounger over. My lips were a hair from his. The warmth of his breath wafted my skin each time he exhaled. I pressed my mouth against his and whispered what every man wanted to hear. "Dinner." And then I popped a kiss and leaned back with a grin.

"You think you're cute, don't you?"

I shrugged and scrunched my face. I mean, I was, so it wasn't that I thought it—I knew it. And, so did Jake. I rolled onto my side and propped myself on my elbow. It was strange to be so comfortable naked around another human being, but I was totally at ease with Jake. He mirrored me, and I noted he didn't seem to feel any embarassment, either.

"Anything, in particular, you'd like to have?"

"Hmm. Something easy. Cheese and crackers, maybe? Some wine?" I sounded like a lush. "I don't get to imbibe much, so it's nice to have a weekend with no homework to worry about or studying to stress over."

He sat up and tossed his legs over the chair, feet on the ground. "Charcuterie it is, but we can definitely do better than just cheese and crackers. I'll add some meats, too."

I did my best not to stare at the chub he had going between his stout thighs. I swore all it took was a bit of wind to get Jake going.

"If you keep staring, you won't have to worry about what you'll be eating."

I burst out laughing, knowing I'd been ogling every inch of him. There was just something delicious about a powerful businessman with a glorious body, who wanted to use it to indulge me with pleasure that I found incredibly attractive.

And watching him prepare a meal for us was more alluring than his body. Every time he moved, everything about him got infinitely better. Other than the whole plane incident, I couldn't find a single thing I didn't love about Jake Hollens. The more time I spent with him, the deeper my heart got involved. There was no chance I'd make it out of this unscathed, yet I couldn't seem to stop myself from going deeper.

⸸

I hated to gather my stuff, knowing Jake was going to take me home. The entire weekend had been perfect, and I didn't want to end it by going back to school. The daily grind of work and class and homework and studying was so far different from what I'd done the last two days that I didn't relish the idea of my real life. But that's what it was—my real life. And I was too close to finishing undergrad to mess it up.

"Peyton, babe, you ready?" Jake called from somewhere down the hall as he approached his bedroom. His expression changed the instant I turned around and he saw my face. "What's wrong?"

I shook my head. "Nothing. I'm just being a baby."

"About what?" Jake captured my hips in his hands and pulled me close, pressing our waists together.

And now I was just pouting. "I've just had a really good weekend."

He brushed my hair from my face and tucked a strand behind my ear. "That's a good thing. In fact, it was the point."

"I know. I just—"

"What?"

I shouldn't have started down this path. "I mean, we had two great days. Now what?"

"We have as many more as you'll give me." His hands left my hips and cupped my jaw. "Is that what you're worried about? You think that this was a one and done sort of thing?"

There wasn't an answer to that question that wouldn't make him mad, so I didn't think responding was the way to go. A non-committal shrug worked nicely.

"Stay."

I chuckled, although not in a funny, ha-ha way. "Yeah, okay." Before I could stop myself, I rolled my eyes like a child and huffed.

Jake stared me down. "I'm not kidding. Stay here. Don't leave."

I pulled away to really see his expression. "Jake, I have a roommate and an apartment. A job. No car. Classes. I can't just stay here."

"Those are logistics, Peyton. I can send someone for your stuff and have it packed and brought here. I'm happy to pay off your lease. Your roommate can stay the duration of the contract without having to worry about her portion. You don't need a job. I have a garage full of cars. And you could still attend classes. It's really quite simple."

I stared at him, not really sure I was processing the words that had just breezed past those beautiful, full lips that I'd spent the majority of the weekend attached to. "And just be what? Your live-in slut?" Granted, that wasn't at all what he'd said, but that was what I'd heard.

He dropped his hold on me and took a step back, wisely. "No, but now that you mention it. It would cut that problem out, as well."

If I reared back any farther, I'd have whiplash and need medical attention. "And what *problem* might that be?" Gone were the tears that had threatened my pity party earlier; I was racing along the border of full-blown fury.

"Sugar. The app. There's no need for you to be on it."

"Except that it's helping me pay my tuition, and with grad school coming up, I can't afford to let any penny slip through the cracks."

His brow furrowed, and his chest heaved. Jake had gotten as worked up as I was for entirely different reasons, and while I was certain he found merit in his argument, I just wanted to slap him. "That's insane. My girlfriend is not going to escort other men around town. First of all, do you have any idea how bad that would look if the press got ahold of it? And secondly, you're *my* girlfriend. I don't share."

It did not escape my attention that his first concern was his image and reputation; the second was our relationship. "I didn't realize we'd established a commitment. And I certainly didn't agree to cut off my income supply to play house with you."

"Play house?"

"Isn't that what this is? You run off to work, and I stay behind, waiting for you to come home to pay attention to me? Maybe give me a scrap of your time on the weekends? Thanks, but no. I already have several of those types of relationships, and they pay me a crapload of money for my attention. I also might mention that they don't ask me to uproot my life and throw it overboard to accommodate their whim!"

He stalked toward me, and with each step in my direction, I took one back until I hit the wall. Jake caged me in with his hands on both sides of my head. I wasn't scared, but I knew he was pissed. "No, Peyton. In case you missed it, I don't want to give you scraps of my time. I want to give you all of me. And as part of that deal, you get all of me. That happens to come with a nice bank account that would allow me to take care of my girlfriend so that she could focus on what's important to her—school."

"I don't want your handouts."

"Fine. But make no mistake, Peyton. I will not share you with another man. I'm a lot of things, but my generosity only goes so far, and it does not include sharing your time."

So now he wanted to dictate what I did with my time as well as where I worked and how I earned a living. "I think you need to take me home." I'd ceased thinking rational thoughts, and all I saw was red.

Without another word, he pushed off the wall and stormed out of the room. I grabbed my backpack and followed, wondering what the hell I'd just done. But I didn't wonder loudly enough to actually open my mouth and apologize or try to find a resolution. I knew the ship was sinking fast, and if I didn't start to bail water quickly, it would go under. However, I was as headstrong as Jake, and it only steeled my resolve to clamp my mouth shut while he drove.

6

JAKE

I should never have left her at the bookstore, not angry like the two of us were. She'd totally mistaken everything I'd tried to say. I didn't want to stifle her; I wanted her to thrive. If I could make it easier for her to do that, then there was no reason for her to object. Or so I'd thought until I removed the emotion from my thought process. And at that point, I might have conceded to an error in judgment. Unfortunately, by the time I'd cooled off, Peyton wasn't within arm's reach or even in my house.

Nor did I have her fucking phone number or any contact information. This time, she'd been smart enough to block me on the app, which left me utterly clueless as to her whereabouts.

And thus, I began my search online. It didn't take

me long to find her—thank you, social media—or that she attended the university not too far from where I'd picked her up and dropped her off.

It was one of the top five schools in the country and also happened to be my alma mater. I shouldn't have been surprised; Peyton was incredibly smart. Although, not smart enough not to have a picture on her profile of her and her girlfriend standing in front of the entrance to the on-campus apartment complex. She'd all but given me a map to her doorstep. I might not know the apartment number, but I had a location and resources at my disposal. I had no idea how she would take my showing up uninvited, but it was clear, she wasn't going to be the first to initiate a conversation since I hadn't heard from her in two days. I had to take matters into my own hands and pray she didn't have me arrested for stalking.

When I first walked into the apartment complex office, I glanced around at the freshly painted walls. The place was so clean that I could see my reflection in every object that surrounded me.

An older man sat at the front desk, reading a maga-zine with his feet propped on the edge. When he looked up, he almost fell out of his chair. "I have to be going blind. You're not Jake *Hollens*, are you?"

I smiled politely. These interactions used to be

really awkward for me, but I took them in stride now. It no longer surprised me that people recognized me out of town or even out of the country, but especially here—my family practically funded the law department at this university and had for generations.

"Yes, I'm here to see Ms. Sanders."

The man's brows rose, but he kept his question to himself. "Oh, umm well... It's against company policy—"

I slid a hundred-dollar bill across the desk. "It's incredibly important I see her."

He leaned forward and swiped the bill, but he didn't give me the information I asked for. I laid four more crisp Jacksons down, and that got him talking.

"She's in apartment eighty-four. Do you want me to show you where it is?" It was an odd request since what he'd just told me was illegal.

I shook my head. "If you'll just point me in the right direction." I let that hang in the air, yet he clearly waited for more information. "I have something for her, and I wanted it to be a surprise." I lifted the small gift bag for him to see.

The man looked intrigued as he nodded, but again, he was smart enough not to ask. "No problem," he said, and I smiled back, thanking him before I walked in the direction he had pointed.

Luckily, I managed to avoid other students along the way. When I reached her door, I took a deep breath before knocking. That's when I was greeted with the sight of a short blonde with blue eyes and a rather foul expression on her face.

"Sorry, I thought this was—"

"Peyton's apartment, yeah, and you're the asshole who treated her like a slut."

My eyes widened. I was at a loss for words. I thought correcting her on her use of the term slut versus whore would be poorly taken, so I kept my mouth shut on that point. "T-That wasn't my intention at all—look, may I speak with her, *please?*"

The woman moved to slam the door in my face, but to both of our surprise, she was stopped by Peyton herself.

Peyton stepped around her friend and crossed her arms over her chest. The pointed stare she gave me would have made my blood run cold if I hadn't thought groveling would ease her sour disposition. "I honestly don't want to talk to you."

I nodded, a pained grimace set firmly on my face. "I know, but I needed you to hear me out."

"You seem to have a bad habit of needing chances to fix things, Jake." It seemed this would be as difficult as rectifying the first mess.

I sighed and gave up the rehearsed speech I had in my head and went for whatever flowed in the moment. "I'm sorry."

"Do those words actually mean anything to you? I mean, you're really good at saying them, but not so great at backing them up."

That stung. It also wasn't true. I didn't apologize to anyone—other than Peyton it appeared. I just wasn't good at dating relationships. I hadn't done much of it and certainly not with anyone I'd actually given a shit about.

I ran my hand through my hair and tried again. "Look, Peyton. I suck at this. The only relationships I'm any good at have dollar signs attached. It's not because I don't want to be better; I just don't have any experience. The feelings I have for you are overwhelming—and clearly, I need to learn how to convey that in a way that computes into care rather than control. I never intended to make you feel like you were anything less than precious."

Her roommate backed away and out of the door, but Peyton didn't ask me inside. She did, however, arch her brows and wait for more. Her eyes softened the longer she stared at me, and I knew, if I chose my words carefully, I might get a second—or rather, *third*— chance.

"I want to date you. Without the app or allowance or tips. A *real* date where we keep in contact with our *actual* phone numbers." I couldn't be more sincere, but it was all I had to offer when I held out my phone for her to take. My emotions were on display for anyone who walked by to see, which for me was actually quite rare.

She looked into my eyes for a moment, which felt closer to hours, before she took the cell from my hand and entered her name and number into my contacts. I smiled, allowing the tension to ease from my back.

I had taken the bracelet out of the box as I walked down the sidewalk and ditched the gift bag in the first trash can I'd seen. The jewelry currently rested in my pocket, and when she handed me the phone, I kept her hand. I slid the device into my pocket in exchange for the bracelet that I wrapped around her slender wrist. Once I'd secured the clasp, I pressed a kissed to her skin.

She looked up at me questioningly, her face flushed from the display of affection.

"I wanted to give it to you when I dropped you off Sunday, but that didn't end how I'd planned it."

Peyton stared at the sparkling white gold on her arm and then her wide eyes turned to mine.

"I bought it for you the first day I was in France.

The stones reminded me of your eyes. I thought about you every day I was gone, and I nearly beat the crap out of my sister for throwing my phone into a fountain when she got mad because it was my only connection to you. But please know, since the day we met, you've been the first thing I thought about when I got up, the last thing I remembered before I went to sleep, and the only thing that keeps me going during the day."

Her eyes filled with surprise, but still, she didn't say a word.

"I've never been in a serious relationship. Once I got out of law school, my dad started grooming me to take over the family business." I dropped her hand to cup her jaw and caress her cheek. The second she leaned in to my touch, I knew she felt for me what I did for her. "I'm going to mess up. I'm going to be absent when you want me present. But please know, I'll keep trying until I get it right—even if it takes me forever."

Her jaw dropped slightly at the proclamation, but it soon closed as I reached down for a kiss. It was short but meaningful. If I could give her my feelings in this single moment I would, just so she could realize how much I cared about her; unfortunately, this would have to be enough.

For now.

7

___

PEYTON

I closed the door behind me and leaned against it, staring off into space, dazed by whatever had just taken place. It was something out of a romance novel, not my real life. But as my fingers traced the smoky-blue stones in the bracelet on my wrist, I realized it was my very own fairytale coming to life.

A goofy expression adorned Sam's face that I imagined mirrored mine. "I don't think Disney could have written that any better."

I tried to scrunch my face into a frown, but I was too giddy to feign disappointment or disgust. Despite my best efforts, little squeals of excitement escaped from my mouth, and I couldn't stop the dance I did with my feet. The energy had to come out, and apparently, it decided it would be in the girliest way possible.

"Well? She tapped her foot and stared at me with wide eyes. "What are you waiting for?" Sam waited for me to understand what she was talking about, but I still wasn't connecting her obvious dots. "Schedule your date already!" Sam was more impatient than I was.

I rolled my eyes and tried to play it cool, nonchalant, but my heart raced a mile a minute. And I was certain that the glazed over way I felt reflected in my expression. "He just left. Don't you think it's too soon?" I'd barely had time to close the door; he probably hadn't even made it to his car yet.

"You spent two solid days with the man. He's seen every inch of you naked, and according to your own account, he's worshipped as much as he's seen and brought you countless orgasms—not to mention a sexy-as-hell nightgown and stunning bracelet." She lifted my hand to show me in case I wasn't sure what she was talking about. "Suffice it to say, I don't think there are any rules of engagement here that you might be breaking." Sam tapped her foot and waited for the realization to hit me.

When I still hadn't dialed Jake's number, she shook her head.

Sam's expression dropped into a blank stare, blinking slowly like I was an idiot and then she inhaled deeply. "You're as daft as he is." She shook her head and tsked. "Two people as beautiful as you guys are should not be destined for each other when neither of you has a clue what you're doing. I swear, it's like the blind leading the blindfolded." She snapped her fingers right in front of my nose. "After everything he just said, I'd bet money he's already texted you. In fact, he's probably waiting in his car, hoping you'll spend the afternoon with him. Wake up, Peyton. For a super smart girl, you sure are clueless." She rolled her eyes with a huff.

I crossed my arms about to make a witty retort when I felt—and Sam heard—the buzzing from my back pocket. She reached around me and snatched the phone before I could stop her. She unlocked it with ease—I needed a new code—smirking as she showed me the message from Jake. I wanted to hate that smug grin, but her being right only meant I was happy.

Jake: Would Saturday at 3pm be good for you? We could walk around the city a bit and explore—just spend time together.

"*Ahh!*" Sam squealed and hopped around in a circle still holding my phone.

I had to forcibly press down on her shoulders just to get a good look at the message.

"Who, Peyton? *Who* says stuff like that? He cannot be heterosexual *and* this romantic at the same time!" She tilted her head from side to side, considering a thought. "Well, if he were a girl, then he could be both, but a man? You need to snatch him up like yesterday, especially since he clearly hasn't realized that not only do you snore when you sleep, but you drool."

I didn't snore—or drool. I did, however, laugh as I waited for her to stop moving. "Weren't you going to castrate him five minutes ago?"

"Yeah, well, that was before I knew he was a modern-day Romeo, Ton-Ton."

Sam had a point. None of my previous boyfriends had ever spoken or acted around me the way Jake did, so I grabbed the phone from my best friend's hand and texted him back.

Me: I'd like that.

I bit my lip. He had this uncanny ability to make me feel things I shouldn't and throw all caution to the wind. Emotionally, I was right back to where I was on our first date. I hated to wait all week to see him, but rushing this wouldn't be a good idea—we'd tried that, *twice*. I made sure to stay caught up on my homework and cleared my work schedule so I was free on Saturday. I was too close to graduation to mess things up now. I'd finished my undergraduate work a year early by taking extra classes and going to summer school every year, and next year I'd be off to law school. I was finally getting closer to my dreams of becoming a prosecutor, and I needed to make sure I stayed focused regardless of how things went with Jake.

In my free time throughout the week, I'd tried on everything I owned in search of the perfect outfit for traipsing around the city. As much as I loved my wedges, they'd likely make me miserable in a short amount of time. I finally decided on jeans, a blue blouse that made my eyes pop, and a pair of white flats. I couldn't help but think that after our weekend together, a casual outing was the perfect way to restart things. There wasn't much trouble we could get into roaming around the city on foot.

I opened the front door and stepped out into the warm air to meet Jake. As soon as I made it to the bottom of the steps, I saw him approaching in the distance. The smile that spread across my face tugged at my lips and made my cheeks ache in the best possible way. His black T-shirt clung to his biceps and stretched across his well-defined chest, and I didn't think a pair of dark-washed jeans had ever looked so tempting on a man. The denim hugged his hips and hung loose in the legs—God, he was hot. I couldn't help but think he'd been smart to suggest a public meeting; otherwise, I'd have a hard time not tearing his clothes from his body.

He leaned in and kissed my cheek before he cooed into my ear. "Hey, Peyton." His breath was warm against my neck, and a chill skirted down my shoulder and then my spine.

"Hi." It appeared I was far more awkward fully dressed than naked and straddling him.

But Jake didn't seem to notice, or maybe he didn't care. He held out his hand, and I took it, the bracelet he gave me still adorning my wrist.

I'd lived in this city my entire life, but Jake still managed to give me a tour that had me on my toes, regaling me with stories about his time in college and the pranks he and his friends had pulled. His face lit up as he reminisced, and I wondered how often he got to do this sort of thing.

The low timbre of his voice calmed my nerves the more I listened to him. We went off paths, finding shortcuts in places I never would've guessed to look, and the longer we walked, the farther I was willing to go—without question. It would be easy to find myself following this man to the end of the Earth.

I clung to his hand, our fingers twined together like it was the most natural thing in the world, and we meandered through the park. I glanced up and realized he'd led us into a small clearing next to the park. It was secluded and virtually untouched by civilization. The wildflowers grew rampant in various shades of pinks and blues and purples. The last time I'd seen something so raw and beautiful was behind Jake's gardens.

Jake chose a spot in the middle of the clearing to sit. The sun peeked through the trees, casting an ethereal glow in a circle. No sooner had I taken a seat next to him than a tiny finch landed on his head.

His eyes grew wide, and his body went stiff. "What the *hell*?" Jake kept his voice low and only moved his eyes.

I moved slowly as not to scare the little feathered friend and got out my phone to take a picture. The sun softened Jake's severe features, and the added effect of the bird perched on his hair was precious.

I lifted my hand near the bird's feet, and surprisingly, it fluttered its wings and hopped onto my finger. The relief on Jake's face made me want to burst out in laughter, but I didn't want to scare my new friend.

"I'm going to call you the finch whisperer from now on."

The bird took flight, and I watched it until I couldn't see it anymore. When I turned back to Jake, he had an easy grin on his lips and a soft tenderness in his eyes. In all the pictures I'd seen of him in the papers and on social media, I'd never witnessed the expression he offered me freely. The press had a knack for making him appear hardened, which worked perfectly for his role at Hollens Industries.

"I always suspected birds were attracted to me." His eyes glittered with humor and crinkled at the sides.

I didn't have a clue what he was talking about, but it was cute. "Oh my God, you sound exactly like Anthony."

His expression immediately turned sour. "That's the worst thing anyone has ever said to me."

I grinned as I sat next to him, watching the breeze move the grass and listening to the leaves rustle in the trees. I leaned into his shoulder, giving him a playful nudge. "You know I'm kidding."

I should have thought about how one of my other "dates" would affect his mood even when the girl he'd been interested in was Jake's sister, not me.

Jake didn't respond and quickly changed the subject. "How's school going?"

I sighed. I didn't really want to talk about any of this, but in the spirit of full disclosure and getting to know him with clothes on, I decided to open up. "Stressful." I tried to give him a look that said I was managing, but I saw the need for more explanation. "My mom has helped out a ton, but I have a lot of student loans." I took a deep breath before saying what came next. I needed him to know where I stood because it could absolutely affect us—it was also the reason I got so upset at his house. "That's why I signed up on the Sugar Daddy app. It's taking chunks off the bottom line at a must faster rate than shifts at the café. And with law school coming up, I need all the help I can get."

Jake hummed in acknowledgment but avoided the topic of the app or my dating other men through it. "What's your major?"

"Pre-law."

He quirked a surprised brow.

I laughed. "What?"

Jake shrugged, and the corner of his mouth ticced up in the slightest hint of a grin. "I don't know. You don't really strike me as the type to be a stickler for the rules."

"When you live with someone like Sam, you learn how to have a little bit of fun. But I certainly don't break any laws—bend them, maybe." I winked.

"*Ah*, the blonde at your apartment?"

I nodded. "Yup, she's the one who introduced me to the app."

Jake laughed. "My friend did the same thing. My dad wants me in a relationship—despite how it might have seemed when you met him—so I appear more stable to stockholders and board members. Secretly, I think he just wants grandkids, and Jessica isn't going to give him any in the near future. Bachelors are easier to pawn off." *At least gorgeous ones like Jake were easy to pawn off—not that Jessica wasn't stunning, too.*

My face soured, thinking of his dad's motivation, causing Jake to chuckle.

"You already know how strict and traditional he is, and my mom's passing only made it worse. It's one of the biggest reasons I caused so much trouble in college. It was the only time I could get away with anything. He's controlled every other moment of my life—ruled with an iron fist." Jake paused for a moment before he seemed to reach a conclusion. "You know Hollens is taking interns in our legal department for the first time in the company's history." He didn't have to tell me; it had been the talk of classes all over campus since the announcement. "You should apply." Jake stared at me, waiting for some sort of response. "I might be able to pull some strings." It was Jake's turn to wink. "You know, since it's my department."

My jaw dropped. "Seriously?"

"You'd make twice what you do on that app, and I wouldn't have to share your time with other men." He smirked at me, but his expression faltered when he noticed my reluctance.

I bit my lip and asked a question I feared having answered. "But why are you offering me this?" I probably should have just seized the opportunity presented and welcomed the chance to get my foot in the door of an enormous corporation before I'd even started law school. But that wasn't who I was. I didn't want to be offered a lucrative position because I'd fucked some guy's brains out in the back seat of a limo after being hired on an escort app, or spent a weekend at his mansion devoid of clothing.

"A couple of reasons. The most important being that you're bright, and I want to snag the best talent out there before the competition does. The second is purely selfish. I don't want to think about your dating other men—real or not—off an app. I've never been good at sharing—it's what makes me a brutal attorney. Call me insecure or territorial or any other adjective, but I want you all to myself." His whispered words tickled my ear as he pulled me into his lap. "That's the way it's supposed to be."

A shiver rolled up my spine, and my chest warmed with pleasure...or maybe that was the space between my thighs. Either or, both worked for me. Jake worked for me. Everything about him brought me to life in the best way possible.

His lips touched my neck, and then he nipped at my ear playfully with his teeth. "I don't want to share you, Peyton. Please?" From any other man, that plea would have been irritating, but from Jake, it was more of a growl, a moan of desperation—desperation I felt just as deeply.

"Promise, no special treatment? I mean other than the hiring me, but after that, it's all business."

"On the clock, yes. I'll agree to that."

"And off the clock?" It was a game I shouldn't play; these types of things had a way of backfiring.

A low rumble came from his chest as he wrapped his arms around me and nuzzled into my neck. "I make no promises about what I'll do to you off the clock. If you agree to be mine, then you're mine. No holds barred. No exceptions." He trailed the tip of his tongue up my neck, and I shifted in his lap to try to ease the growing need between my legs.

I pushed back a bit to see his face and tried to give him a reprimanding look but failed miserably. My cheeks grew heated when he held my gaze and his hand trailed up my inner thigh. Around the top of my leg and to my backside, his fingers blazed a path until he cupped my ass in both hands. In seconds, he'd situated me so I straddled him, and he'd captured my protest in a panty-dropping kiss.

The more his hands roamed, the less I cared about where we were. I lost myself in the sounds of nature and Jake's finding pleasure in my body. His fingers slipped beneath the waistband of my pants, and I gasped when he unbuttoned the fly. Jake leaned me back and worked my jeans down my legs, taking my panties with them. He teased my clit, his touches lighter than the bird's feathers as he explored. *Every. Fucking. Crevice.* He cut off my gasps for air with another searing kiss, slipping his tongue into my mouth the second he inserted a single digit into my wet, waiting, and wanting pussy.

"*Mmm.*" The sound of his groan removed any care I had left in the world.

At this point, if we got caught, all the ridicule and embarrassment would be worth the feel of him against me again.

I didn't care that the blouse was new or that there

was a twig digging into my back. Not even the pebbles that I'd have to pick out of my skin deterred me. If anything, they made the experience even more enticing, more feral. I dug my nails into his skin when he added pressure on my cunt. Rubbing my clit with his thumb, he inserted another finger. My back arched, and I shifted my hips beneath his grip, urging him to move faster.

Jake refused to give me what I craved, and instead, teased me further as he trailed kisses down every inch of bare skin he could find until his mouth joined his fingers in a symphony of pleasure. I panted for air or release—I needed one or the other. Tremors wracked my body in his relentless pursuit of my orgasm. His fingers. His tongue. His mouth. Up, down, in, out. I couldn't tell where one started and another ended. And then he curled his fingers into my G-spot, and I nearly lost my mind.

"Oh...Oh, God. Jake...*fuck*." I couldn't get out a complete sentence to save my life, and I'd long since passed caring about how loud I'd become. "I'm gonna *come*." My entire body flushed, and an intense euphoria rolled through me from toe to head and back. I shuddered, riding the waves his tongue provided until I couldn't move.

Sex with this man felt like we were shattering the very fabric of the universe.

Jake crawled up my body from between my legs with a bright smile. He licked his lips before pulling me into another kiss, allowing me to taste myself. There was something alluring and edgy about enjoying myself on his lips. It was so easy to forget the world around us whenever Jake was near.

As the sun began to set, Jake helped me with my jeans and then pulled me up. "Come on; it's getting dark."

It had started to get chilly out, so I used that as an excuse to walk closer to him—not that I needed one. That much was evident by the obvious bulge in Jake's pants, but his smile and carefree demeanor convinced me that he had been content just to make me scream today.

This man was going to be the death of me.

And I wasn't so sure I minded.

8

JAKE

It had been a couple of months since we'd officially started dating, and I couldn't have asked for things to have been more perfect. The lawyers at the firm had taken Peyton under their wings, and she'd dove headfirst into learning, soaking up everything she could. She took the job seriously, and she hadn't wavered from the "no special treatment" stipulation. That was incredibly important to her, and it was her top priority. Most days, I wasn't even on her radar when she was in the building.

At first, I'd thought she had buckled down because of the paparazzi flare-up. We'd been spotted leaving the park—after our reckless romp in the woods—and the hounds had figured out that the city's most eligible bachelor was off the market. They had a field day with the fact that Peyton was a college student, and then when it surfaced that she had been awarded one of the three coveted intern positions, rumors headlined every gossip rag on the newsstand. But it hadn't taken the press long to fall for her the way I had, but the spin they put on the rags-to-riches love story had my father reeling.

It also resulted in my getting far more phone calls of a personal nature from him than I ever had in the past. Every time Peyton and I attended an event, our photos were splashed on the front page of the lifestyle section or featured in a news bit. Last night we'd attended a charity gala, and I'd been anticipating the ass-chewing I was currently receiving.

"What's wrong with you, Jake? There are certain things expected from you as the heir to Hollens Industries. You've known this for years." He continued to rant while I leaned back in my chair and twirled a pen between my fingers. "All this will do is invite every poor girl from the wrong side of the tracks to come play in our neighborhood, son. I won't stand for it. It makes the whole family look bad."

I couldn't stifle the chuckle that passed my lips. "You're kidding, right? Do you realize what a positive effect the publicity has had for the corporation?" I refused to let him interrupt me when he attempted to cut in. "Our sales are up twenty percent since the papers started reporting on my relationship."

"You have no proof that's from media coverage." My father was a stubborn old goat, and I knew he wouldn't willingly see anything he didn't want to.

I'd also determined that he'd gotten so used to his misery since Mom died that he almost relished it. Over the years, I'd become a huge part of that company, and while misery loved me, I didn't reciprocate that affection. My father could either get on board or lose another loved one in the process.

"What else would you attribute it to, Dad? We haven't started any new campaigns, we are in what is normally our slowest season of the year, and nothing else has made headlines. So, you tell me what brought on the influx in business."

"I'm not arguing with you, Jake. My friends—our business associates—they're asking questions." And there it was—the real reason he was in an uproar. "End it. *Now.*" Thankfully, his yelling couldn't be heard beyond the receiver on my phone, although I wasn't certain I'd be able to hear at all after this conversation.

I slammed my hand on my desk, not that he could hear or see how angry he'd made me. Despite sound-proof walls, I refused to scream at my father. That was something I had been raised not to do. "No." I bit back the resentment and tried like hell to keep my tone even. "I'm a grown man. You have no right to tell me who I can or can't be with."

This had been one of many reasons for avoiding the dating scene since college. My father believed he got a say in who I loved. No, that wasn't true. My father didn't believe that I had a right *to* love. My obligation was to the family, and that was a business transaction. He expected me to marry to further the company. But he hadn't always been blinded by that narrow-minded belief, just since my mom had passed away.

"Your little fling is already having negative consequences for the family. Jamison Judge—"

"Has a single daughter you've been trying to pawn off on me since grad school. Fuck Jamis—"

"Watch your mouth son, Jamison's a good man."

"And Peyton's a good girl." I didn't say anything that wasn't true.

"She's already ruining the family name!" He needed to lower his voice before I blew my top.

I scoffed. "What century do you live in?" My disrespectful tone and argumentative word choice would only serve to keep this insanity going, but I couldn't stop. "Arranged marriages are a thing of the past. People choose who they want to marry, *Dad!*"

"Jake!"

I pulled the phone from my ear to glare at it the way I would him if he were actually in front of me. I'd be damned if he was going to reprimand me for dating someone he didn't deem worthy. "The conversation's over. You're not going to dictate who I'm in a relationship with. Plain and simple." I was about to hang up when his next words caused me to pause.

"Is she worth your inheritance?"

I couldn't believe what I was hearing, and as such, I couldn't formulate a response before he dug that knife a little deeper into my back and twisted.

"One phone call to the legal department is all it will take to remove your name from the will and the corporation."

I laughed, highly unamused. "Talk about scandal. You think the press has been all over Peyton and me? What do you think they'll do with a story about your cutting your only son out of your will because she didn't come from the right bloodline or the right part of town?"

He stumbled over a response, so I kept going.

"I won't be the one embarrassed or exposed as a miser. I'll win over hearts across the globe for choosing love over money. I'd have my pick of positions at any international hotel chain, and you know it. Don't push me on this. I've got the key to the closet where you keep all of your skeletons."

"You'd never embarrass your family that way."

I smirked. Oh, how wrong he was. "Try me." There was one thing I'd learned since I'd met Peyton, and that was, she trumped everything. Money, power, prestige—I'd throw it all away to secure her place at my side. There was nothing my father could say that would change that.

"Are you threatening me, boy?" He hadn't used that term to cut me down since high school.

The difference between then and now was that I no longer cared. I'd worked my ass off for him and this company, and if whom I chose to sleep with became a barrier in that path, then I'd switch paths. But this shit stopped today.

"And don't think I'm not well aware of your intentions behind those meetings in Australia and Paris. Jessica was perfectly capable of handling them on her own, but you couldn't stand the thought of my seeing Peyton after you met her. It won't happen again. Know that now."

He didn't say anything, but I could hear the heavy pant of his labored breath in the background and knew he was still on the line.

"I will always give Hollens one-hundred percent

of my attention on the clock. I'll do what is necessary to get the job done. I *will not* cut Peyton out to do it."

When my father refused to respond, I hung up, knowing I'd won this round in a war that would likely never end. It wasn't what I wanted, but if he couldn't get on board with my personal choices, then he needed to get off the train. We didn't have to be buddies for me to be good at my job.

I'd barely hung up the phone, much less disguised my irritation, when a knock sounded on my door.

"Come in," I barked out, and my door crept open.

Peyton peeked her head in, and I instantly regretted not watching my tone.

I grinned at the sight of the pink blush that flushed her cheeks. "Hey, beautiful." Before I had the words out of my mouth, I'd stood and rounded my desk.

She'd keep me at arm's length while we were inside Hollens Industries, but that didn't mean I couldn't inhale her sweet scent and think about how nice it would be to have my way with her when we left here tonight.

Her spine was straight and her shoulders pulled back. Peyton was the epitome of professional, a fact my father would delight in if he'd ever spent any time with her. "I have the report Jessica filed on the lawsuit in Australia. She asked me to bring it to you."

I nodded, stepped closer, and took the file. Before she could pull back, I grabbed her wrist and tugged her front to my chest. In one swift motion, I tossed the folder onto the ever-growing pile on my desk, while simultaneously snaking my arm around her waist to prevent her escape. Peyton hesitated when I nuzzled my nose into her neck and nipped at her flesh, making her skin pebble.

"Jake, someone is going to see us." She whispered into my ear without thinking about what her heated breath did to me.

My dick twitched in my slacks, and I turned us in order to kick the door closed and lock it. "Better?"

Her fingers dug into my sides, and her mewl did nothing to dissuade me. "We can't do this here." Peyton's mouth said one thing, but her body said another as she sank into my embrace. "Jake..."

I'd heard her moan those four letters in a ballad of pleasure more times than I could count. Using them to deter my pursuit wouldn't work. And when her nails scratched at the back of my head, her fingers tangling in my hair, I knew she was one well-placed grind away from living out my greatest fantasy.

With her ass in my hands, I rolled my hips against her center. She clutched my nape with one hand and my waist with the other in a desperate attempt to remain strong. I pulled out all the stops and kissed her just behind the ear in the only place—next to her pussy—that she couldn't resist. Her hands began to roam, and when I pulled back, heat pooled in her eyes. Her pupils were dilated, and her nostrils flared.

My lips met hers in a soft exchange, although it was nothing more than a peck to entice her. "Mhm, so this is when you finally make my fantasy come true?"

Her perfectly sculpted brows dipped. "Oh, is your secretary joining us?" A devilish grin tugged at the corners of her pouty mouth.

Not only was I not interested in a threesome, but my secretary was pushing seventy-years old and a grandmother of fourteen. "I should spank your ass for that little comment."

"Would that be before or after you bend me over your desk?" Yeah, Peyton knew exactly which fantasy I referred to. She glanced at the furniture in question, and then she tugged at my chin with her fingers. "All those perfectly organized files and stacks and cases." There was a place for everything, and it was all in meticulous order. "Is it worth having to reorganize all that just to have your way with me in your office?" Peyton thought she was teasing me, that I wouldn't really do it, especially not in the middle of the day when the entire staff was right outside that locked door.

Peyton blew softly into my ear, causing my attention to focus on the blood rushing to my dick. And when the tip of her tongue traced my lobe, I nearly shouted.

"That would be a resounding yes. I'll have one of the interns organize whatever ends up on the floor."

Her eyes went wide when I reached for the buttons on her pressed, white blouse. And her mouth parted when I released the zipper on the side of her brown pencil skirt. I stepped back to see Peyton modeling the sexiest white-lace bra and matching thong I'd ever seen. But it was the tortoiseshell heels that did me in.

"Take them off." I jerked my head in the direction of her lingerie, and she knew without further instruction exactly what I'd meant.

And as she teased me with her own little dance, I didn't hesitate to unbuckle my belt and undo the fly on my slacks. I'd outlined this particular dream for her in detail. Peyton knew what I wanted, how I planned to take it, and exactly what I expected of her. And my girl did *not* disappoint.

She kicked her pile of clothing aside, turned to face the desk, and spread her legs. I'd never seen her move as slowly as she did when she bent at the waist, pressing her bare breasts to the wood, and then reached out to hold on to each edge. She turned her head to the side and closed her eyes, but I didn't miss the tilt of her lips. And when I glanced down, I didn't miss the gleam of her wet pussy. Peyton was as turned on as I was.

I reached into my boxers, pulled my erection free, and stepped up behind her. My hand landed at the swoop of her waist, and my fingers curled around her hipbone. Whether I'd startled her, or she'd wanted me as much as I did her, I didn't know, nor did I care. Her ass shifted as she offered her sweet cunt for my taking. The head of my cock nudged her clit, but she didn't move. I slid my shaft through her soft folds, lubricating myself in her juices. I could smell her scent, and fuck if I didn't want to devour her.

Her chest heaved with anticipation, and when I plunged into her warmth, her eyes flew open, and she clenched the desk, turning her knuckles white. But I didn't give her what she wanted—or what I needed—right away. I savored the feel of her surrounding me and enjoyed the soft, wet heat.

A rumble came from her chest in what could only be the start of a growl. "Jake..." Her hedonistic tone set me into motion. Peyton hissed as I withdrew and then gasped when I dove back in.

"Shit." I held still. This would end almost as fast as it began if I didn't get my head in the game.

"You all right?"

There would never be a time that I was inside Peyton's pussy that I wasn't a hell of a lot better than *all right*. It was fucking euphoric, and I'd live there if I could. I wonder what that would do for the family name. "Yeah." I breathed the word more than I actually spoke it.

I started slowly in an attempt to savor every second we were together, but that little gasp, the shiver that ran down her spine, and then the way she moaned, "please" set me off. "Fuck, Peyton, I didn't think you could get any tighter."

She didn't respond, and that didn't work for me. I needed to hear her. I wanted to know she felt as good as I did. Peyton was nothing if not vocal—she never disappointed. But her eyes had drifted closed again, and I wanted them open. Along with her mouth.

I slammed into her, and she fulfilled both of my silent requests, but there was still no noise. Pounding into her again, she bit her lip. On the third slam, she squeezed her eyelids shut.

I slapped her ass, a bright-red handprint appearing immediately. "Baby, I want to hear you."

She shook her head, and I smacked her ass again. Harder this time.

I drove into her over and over in a relentless pursuit of her affirmation. "Peyton..." I watched as she chewed on her lip, trying desperately not to utter a peep. "They can't hear you." Nor could they hear my balls slapping against her wet cunt.

And my girl came to life, her face lifted from the desk, and her back arched in the most gorgeous curve I'd ever seen. "Yes, Jake." She panted, and I used her current position to grab hold of her pert breast to tweak her nipple. "Right there." Peyton was beautiful and all mine; I'd never give her up. "Don't stop." ...Even if she couldn't complete a sentence with more than two words in it.

I loved that my cock nearly rendered her speechless and almost made her forget her name. But there was one name she never forgot.

"Jake."

I laid against her back, flattening her once again to the desk. I wanted to kiss her lips or her soft skin. I'd love to trail my fingers along the dip in her side or the swell of her ass. But I was too far gone in her pussy to do anything other than fuck the hell out of her. "God, you're amazing," I muttered into her hair as I rolled my hips into her ass.

She clawed at my arms, desperate for any part of me to hold on to. Finally, Peyton rounded her hands on my forearms, and I thrust into her with all I had. "I'm going to come, Jake."

I barely heard her warning, but I would have felt it regardless. Her internal temperature rose several degrees, her muscles clenched, and she bit into my bicep as her orgasm ripped through her. And mine stampeded right behind it. When the last of me had been spent, I laid on top of her. Her limbs were as limp as mine, and her lips turned up in a sated grin.

"I think I love you, Jake Hollens." Her eyes fluttered closed, and she hummed with satisfaction.

Her words should have freaked me out.

Any other man would panic.

My heart hammered so hard in my chest, I thought it might pound out in excitement. She'd never uttered those words, but I'd felt them for weeks. I'd known she was different when I got on that plane; I just had no idea how strongly I would connect with her when I returned home. Never in my wildest dreams did I believe I'd win her back. And the fantasies coming to life were just an added bonus. Peyton was the prize.

"That word doesn't do justice to what I feel for

you." It might have sounded like a line, but it was one of the most truthful things I'd ever said.

She peered back over her shoulder with a raised brow, and I eased off her and stood. "Oh, really?"

"I can't explain something I don't understand, Peyton. I just know it's the truth the way I know the grass is green or the sky is blue. It just *is*."

She huffed and righted herself to perch her naked ass on the edge of my desk—a desk that was utterly destroyed, although I didn't think now was the time to bring that up. "That was vague." Her chest was red and had creases indented in her skin from lying on top of file folders.

I laughed at her serious expression—if she could see the zigzags across her breasts, she'd find humor in it, too—and zipped up my pants. She dropped her attention to the floor as she began to collect her clothes she'd kicked aside. I couldn't pull my eyes from her firm ass when she squatted in her fuck-me heels, but it was watching her step into her prissy thong that had me grumbling about leaving work for the day that made her laugh. This girl had me wrapped, and I loved every minute of it.

"You're like cocaine." I grabbed her hips and tried to pull her to me. "I get high off you."

She giggled and shook her head as she buttoned

her shirt. "Have you been Googling pick-up lines for college girls?" Peyton kissed my lips lightly and patted my cheek like a child. "I just told you I love you. You don't need cheesy lines, Jake."

I looked at the painting on the wall beside her head instead of looking into her eyes. "No, what would give you that idea?" There was a significant difference in our ages, but that didn't mean I needed help keeping Peyton's attention. And I sure as hell hadn't turned to the internet to up my game.

Peyton snorted, and I pinched her nose lightly in retaliation.

"I didn't know I was dating a pig?"

Peyton's eyes went round like saucers as she tried to scoff, but it came out as an exaggerated huff. She smacked my hand and glared at me, although it lacked any real intensity. I raised my brows innocently.

She slid her skirt up her legs and zipped it on the side, righting her clothing. "Are you calling me fat?"

"Wha- no, of course not. I was just saying that you're good enough to eat." I wagged my brow with insinuation. All she had to do was lose the panties, and I'd show her just what I meant. "You know, I really do love how you women like to twist words."

She narrowed her eyes and cocked her head as she tried not to laugh. "Oh, so not only are you sexist, but you also want to slaughter me and serve me up for dinner, *hmm?*"

"Yes, *Samantha,* I believe that's exactly what I said. I eat only the *best* kind of meat."

Her best friend and I continued to debate the morality of animal consumption. It was a good thing she thought I was endearing because that was the only thing that had kept Sam from tearing off my balls and stuffing them down my throat when I argued every point of her pro-plant lifestyle.

Fully dressed, Peyton once again looked the part of the perfect employee, while I looked the part of a sexual harassment charge facing justice. But I didn't care. She wasn't going to rat me out, and I sure as hell wasn't going to complain to human resources.

She stepped to me, put her hands on my hips, and pressed her lips to mine.

"You know I love you, too, don't you?" There wasn't a doubt in my mind she had known for quite some time, but I needed to be certain.

Her hands moved up to my chest, and I draped my arms around her waist. "Is that a statement or a question?"

"I love you."

She popped a quick peck on my lips. "I know you do."

"Move in with me." I hadn't mentioned it since that weekend that had ended in disaster. "Please." But that didn't mean I had changed my mind. "I hate the days that I don't wake up next to you. And it's silly to have your mail going to another address just to prove a point."

Her lease was up at the end of the summer. Sam had taken a job in California after graduation so that was no longer an excuse. I wanted to take care of her. I didn't want to be her sugar daddy; I wanted to be her everything.

"Jake..."

I shook my head. "No. Don't do that." I didn't want that pitiful stare that said she thought I was lonely. "I'm serious, Peyton."

Her expression contorted into something unreadable. Instead of calling her on it, I waited. And then I realized she was scheming.

"What's in it for me?" Her tone was as playful as the glimmer in her eyes.

I pressed my still semi-hard dick against her. "I think I just gave you a taste of what you can count on daily."

She tapped her finger on her lips like she was thinking. "I don't think Gwen will care for us shacking up together." She was wrong about that; Gwen had helped me pick out the ring that currently sat in my jacket pocket.

"What if I could assure you that Gwen would give us her blessing?" I let Peyton go and took the steps away from her that were necessary to reach my coat by the door.

Peyton cocked her hip out to the side and crossed her arms under her pert breasts; I had to bite my tongue to keep from growling. "Then I'd say yes...if you could assure me that Gwen gave us her blessing."

I reached into the pocket, pulled out the box, and kept it covered with my hand. Peyton eyed my fist, but she didn't ask what I was up to. And when I got within arm's reach, she started to put her hands on me. But when I dropped down onto one knee, her fingers flew to her mouth, covering her lips and masking her tiny gasp.

It was fast. I knew it was. But I'd never been so certain about anything in my life. I wanted Peyton in my home, and I wanted her there with my last name.

"Will you marry me?"

She didn't hem. She didn't haw. There wasn't so much as a quibble—or a word. Peyton nodded and threw her arms around my neck as I stood. Tears rushed down her cheeks, but when I pulled back to kiss my fiancé's lips, I recognized that they were tears of joy. I barely got the ring on her finger before her palms covered my jaw. That was the kind of kiss I wanted for the rest of my life—one filled with passion and all from Peyton.

Peyton didn't care about the ring. In fact, I had to force her to look at it instead of making out with me, which took incredible resolve on my part.

"It's beautiful." She was beautiful. Our life together would be beautiful. That stone was just a rock.

I wiped the tears from her cheeks with my thumbs. "Thank Gwen. You'd hate to see what I would have picked out without her assistance." I laughed, and she giggled with me. "But needless to say, she gives her blessing."

Peyton blushed and cast her gaze down.

I tipped her chin up to see what had suddenly changed her mood. The timidness was unfamiliar. "What's wrong?"

She batted her dark lashes, and I knew I was in trouble. "Can we go home early?" Not once had she asked for any preferential treatment—*ever*. In fact, she worked overtime and volunteered for every crap job any of the other attorneys threw at her to overcompensate for her relationship with me.

I didn't bother answering that question. I shut

down my computer, grabbed my jacket, and then took Peyton's hand. As we passed my secretary, I told her Peyton and I would see her on Monday and asked her to have Travis—Peyton's friend and one of the three interns—clean up the mess on my desk. She didn't seem the least bit surprised and simply waved us on.

And then, I took Peyton home to show her just how fucking much I loved her and how excited I truly was for her to join the Hollens family.

JAKE

*A*pparently, all it took for my father to fall in love with Peyton was recognizing that I'd give it all up for her—everything. He'd had the same conversation with his father about my mother, but I'd never known that part of their story. No one had told us as kids that our mom came from the wrong side of the tracks and didn't have the breeding worthy of the Hollens' family name. I didn't learn that truth until after I'd proposed, knowing I had risked it all.

My dad stood at my side as my best man as Peyton walked down the aisle toward us. Jessica and Sam led the way, but I only had eyes for my bride. And God was she stunning. Happiness radiated from her cheeks and danced in her eyes. Never in my life had I thought when I signed up for an escort app that I'd meet the woman who would become my wife and hopefully, one day, the mother of my children. Yet, here she was, and it was happening. All of my dreams were coming true.

I didn't remember anything about the ceremony other than her finally saying, "I do." Oh, and the kiss. That would be one I remembered for a lifetime. The reception flew by in a blur with the hundreds of people who'd been invited and attended.

It wasn't until I had my wife at my side on the corporate jet that I was finally able to take a deep breath and relax for our honeymoon.

Peyton buckled her seatbelt and let out a heavy sigh. "Whew." She feigned a swipe at her brow. "That was a close call."

My brow furrowed, and I wondered what had happened that I'd missed. I hadn't let her out of my sight. She'd literally been on my arm since we met at the altar. Even when we'd changed clothes, I was there —and took full advantage of her nudity in the time that was allotted—at her side.

"What's wrong?" Panic laced my tone as I worried over what had upset her.

She thumbed over her shoulder toward the limo we'd just left. "For a minute there, I wondered if you'd slam the door in my face and take off to the jet without me. It was a close call." Peyton didn't crack a smile or even look my direction. She kept situating herself in the seat while my mouth hung open.

When she finally burst out laughing, my shoulders sagged in relief.

"I'm never going to live that down, am I?"

She popped a kiss on my lips and leaned back with a bright smile. "Never is a really long time, but...*no.*"

That was okay. I had an eternity to try.

The End

Click or scan the QR code to check out
other books by Mila Hart

ACKNOWLEDGMENTS

Kristie and Stephie (aka Mila Hart) want to extend a special thank you to Paging through the Days, bloggers, and readers who take chances on new authors. You have so many options, and Mila is forever grateful that you picked *Sugar*!

It all started with two best friends and a whole lot of dirty ideas...

MILA HART is your go-to for cheeky, steamy, and seriously spicy reads. We're all about quick, hot stories that get your heart racing and leave you wanting more —but here's the twist: we give you both the heat and the story.

With tons of deliciously sexy tales in the works, get ready for the perfect mix of plot and passion—because we're just getting started!

Check us out at:

www.authormilahart.com

www.ingramcontent.com/pod-product-compliance
Lightning Source LLC
Chambersburg PA
CBHW071434130726
47997CB00006B/2081